TAKESHITA DEMONS
THE
FILTH LICKER

CRISTY BURNE
ILLUSTRATED BY SIKU

F
FRANCES LINCOLN
CHILDREN'S BOOKS

CHAPTER ONE

"Cait, are you still there?" I could hear breathing on the other end of the phone, but Cait's voice had disappeared, cut off halfway through a sentence. "Hello?" It was dark outside, late on the night before school camp, and I had a bad feeling in my gut that was cutting like knives. I was supposed to be packing shirts and shoes and lucky charms to take to camp, but I hadn't even opened my case.

The phone crackled. "Sorry," Cait whispered. "I had to go quiet. I'm supposed to be in bed. Dad'll freak if he finds me up this late."

So she was still there. Still OK. Relief prickled down my arms.

"What's up?" she asked. "Why are you calling so late?"

I swallowed. "It's about camp," I began. "I've got this feeling..."

Cait didn't hesitate. "I know," she said. "Me too."

I grinned despite the churning in my belly. Of course Cait would understand. She'd been with me through everything, helping me break into our school and rescue my brother, making friends with a half-dragon water-woman, even standing up to Mrs Okuda after she'd become a child-eating nukekubi demon. Since the night we'd met the demons, Cait and I had been virtually inseparable. Unlike Mrs Okuda and her head.

"I've been thinking," Cait continued. "About camp. I think we're going to need a few extra things...."

I listened, on the edge of my bed.

"But it's hard to know," she said. "For a start, I think I'll take two pairs, then I can wear one at dinner or whatever, and have the other if Mr Lloyd makes us go hiking. Are you taking two? "

"What? What are you talking about?"

The phone went silent. "Jeans," Cait said. "What are *you* talking about?"

"Demons." I hissed the word into the phone, as if a demon might be listening outside my door that very second. "At camp."

The phone stayed silent.

"Cait?" What was going on over there? Maybe she wasn't safe after all….

But then Cait's voice came rattling into my ear. She sounded tired. "Demons again, Miku? I thought you'd finished with that."

"But…"

"Mrs Okuda has gone," she said. "Mr Lloyd is back. You've got to give all this demon stuff a rest. We're off to camp tomorrow. No spooks or flying heads there."

"But we'll be all alone out there." School camp in the countryside. Cabins without locks. Woods on three sides and a hungry river out the back. Plus a long, lonely walk to the toilets every night. My guts twisted like snakes. "Anything could find us."

Cait snorted. "You worry too much. Focus on the good stuff. A whole week without homework."

"But what about that smell?" I sniffed, but I couldn't smell it now, which was a pleasant change. At school, in the library, on the bus. We'd been smelling it everywhere, something animal and musty, like a cross between wet dog and monkey droppings.

"Look…" There was a sigh and some shuffling. "I've gotta pack. Can we talk tomorrow?"

Tomorrow wouldn't help the feeling in my gut tonight, but perhaps Cait was right. Maybe we would be safe at camp. Maybe things would get better if we were further from home and away from our school, where everything had started. Still I delayed, feeling the hot phone burn into my ear. But I couldn't wait for ever. "OK. Sure. Tomorrow would be good."

"Great. So two pairs?"

I sighed. "Yeah. Two's probably enough."

So much for inseparable. Cait was now quick to change the subject if I wanted to talk supernatural spirits. Back when the nukekubi had invaded our school, Cait had believed me, defended me, even risked her neck for me. But maybe demons just weren't her thing any more. I was beginning to feel as if there was a forest between us, and it was growing.

That night I tried to stay busy, putting things in my case and taking them out again. Eventually, after everything was packed for the fiftieth time, I went to bed.

I lay there for ages, but I didn't sleep. The sick feeling in my stomach grew steadily worse, and from inside the walls of my room I could hear the rise and fall of something wailing. My bag was packed. The camp bus would leave in just a few hours. But something, somewhere, had already begun.

CHAPTER TWO

At school on Monday morning I watched the good seats disappear, one after the other. Mr Lloyd was heaping luggage into the bottom of the camp bus and Ms Jackson, our deputy head, was ticking off names as kids scrambled into the bus.

I searched for Cait, scanning for her face as the rest of our school streamed through the gates and into their classrooms. They pointed at our bus, eyes envious, but I would have swapped places with them in an instant.

Don't get me wrong. School camp would have been great at any other time. No lessons, no tests, no homework for a week. You hang out with friends all day and all night and stay up too late telling ghost stories. But this time it was different. I could feel something evil was brewing. The air tasted metallic and my gut felt as if it was filled with tiny knives. Plus today was an unlucky day on the calendar. The timing just couldn't have been worse.

The night before, I'd packed good-luck charms into every spare pocket of my case: my maneki-neko keychain, with its snow-white cat to bring money and luck; a bright red omamori charm from when Dad took us to Kyoto to watch the cherry blossoms; even the wooden ear-pick Baba gave me on my seventh birthday, the one with a tiny daruma doll dangling off the top.

Baba had told me to think of a wish and draw in one of the daruma's eyes, then to draw in his other eye when the wish came true. I'd wished for Mum to buy me a soft-serve macha ice-cream, and my wish had come true almost that same day. Now both his eyes were inky black and my ice-cream was gone. But still, it couldn't hurt to have him with me.

"Miku!" Cait's voice carried across the car park. She came scrambling in my direction, hair sticking out from under a baseball cap and her case jumbling alongside.

She'd been my best friend ever since I'd arrived in England and started at this school, more than a year ago now. It was just that lately I'd felt as if she was changing. And phone calls like last night's made the feeling worse.

"Bus was late," she puffed, hauling her case up the curb so it bounced into the air. "Thought I wasn't going to make it."

I grinned, forgetting the ice in my stomach. Some things never changed. Cait's bus always seemed to be late. "Come on!"

We carted our cases to where Mr Lloyd was waiting, then skipped to the front door of the bus.

"Miku Takeshita. Cait O'Neill." Ms Jackson looked over her glasses, scanning her list with one finger. She was dressed in jeans and a T-shirt. I hardly recognised her. "Your luggage in the hold? Permission forms? Good." She ticked off our names. "In you get. We're going to have a terrific week."

But it didn't start out terrific. There were hardly any seats left, and nowhere Cait and I could sit together, which meant we'd have to sit miles apart, and probably next to some kid who would vomit all the way. Or...

I looked down the bus and saw two free seats, both aisle seats, one in front of the other. Then I saw who was sitting in the window seats next to those aisle seats, and I shuddered. No way was I sitting there.

"Hey, Miku Mouse!"

I grimaced. It was Alex. And behind him, his best mate, Oscar. Alex took every chance to tease me almost every day of school. If it wasn't my name, it was my accent, or my hair, or the contents of my lunchbox…. I scrunched up my shoulders and tried to pretend I hadn't seen him.

"You wanna sit next to me?" he called out. "You can sit right here."

I sneaked another look. Alex was patting the seat next to him, and leering like a goofball. Oscar was hanging over the seat behind Alex, holding back his laughter. They had a window seat each, and both of the seats next to them were still free.

Cait and I looked up and down the bus for other options. I screwed up my face. "Perhaps they'll move if we ask them nicely?"

As if. We didn't have a hope.

"Miku Mouse," Alex crowed. "Come on, I saved you a place." He thumped the seat next to him and Oscar hooted in response.

"This one's for you, O'Neill." Oscar patted his seat for Cait.

"Ugh." Cait looked desperate.

We scanned the rest of the bus for spare seats. But there was nothing. I made a face at Cait.

"Ugh," she said again. But what could we do?

Cait sat with Oscar and I sat with Alex, squeezing as far away from him as possible. I don't think he'd actually expected me to sit with him. He went red and shuffled right against the window. Served him right. Then he hardly said a word, just put on his iPod and started drumming on the windowsill. Behind me I could hear Oscar doing the same.

I twisted round to check on Cait. She was perched so far on the edge of her seat that she was practically in the aisle.

"Better than nothing?" I asked.

She nodded. "I guess."

"How long's the trip?"

"Four hours? Five? Something like that."

I groaned, swinging back to face the front of the bus. It was moments like these when I wished I really did have superpowers. Then I could maybe make this bus trip disappear.

Apparently, if you can believe a demon with a woman's head and a snake's body, I had some sort of special powers. Not that there'd been any sign of them, certainly none that I'd seen.

Of course, she was probably just being nice. She called herself the Woman of the Wet and said she'd been sent by Zashiko, my family ghost, to keep us

13

safe. That bit might have been true, but if she'd been right about the powers, I'd only have to blink and this bus ride would be over. Instead I had to spend half the day sitting next to Alex. Great.

I slumped in my chair, thinking of Zashiko and Baba and the house we'd shared in Japan. There'd been no demon trouble back then. Outside the bus, the world changed from houses and cars to fields and trees. We were on our own now. I tried to think positive. Sometimes being on your own was better than being with things that wanted to eat you. Bunches of cows flicked by and the air grew warmer inside the bus.

Alex was still drumming on the windowsill, and doing such a bad job I wanted to reach over and make him stop. The space between my eyes was beginning to ache, so I closed them and tried to think of something that didn't involve getting hunted by supernatural enemies or being trapped in a bus seat with Alex, the human drum machine. With my eyes shut, I could feel the engine roar and the road rock beneath me. I pretended I was far away, on an aeroplane maybe.

Seconds later I woke, heart pounding. The ground was shaking and that smell was back – the musky, unwashed, animal smell.

"Move it, Miku Mouse!" Something loomed over me, tentacles dangling from its ears.

I sat up, whirling round with my hands up to protect my face. I was ready to fight, ready to run.

"Now. Like today if possible." The thing gave my seat a shake, iPod still hanging from its ears.

I blinked, then looked again. It was Alex. The bus had stopped outside a tiny shop and most of the kids were already filing out, traipsing off to buy chocolates and lollies, or joining the queue for the loo.

"Where are we?" I turned, checking for Cait.

"You were asleep," she grinned, standing behind me in the aisle. "For hours."

"Snoring is more like it." Alex shook the seat again. "Now move!"

I blinked and looked around. Something didn't feel right.

"Ice-cream?" Cait asked.

"Sure." I nodded vaguely, heaving myself out of the seat.

"Finally!" Alex complained. "Do you mind?" He and Oscar jumped into the aisle and squeezed past us, jostling each other off the bus.

I peered out of the window as Cait and I moved

towards the exit. "Where are we?" We were the last kids on the bus and my voice seemed unnaturally loud.

"Some town." Cait shrugged, following me down the aisle.

But it was hardly a town. I paused on the top step of the bus, looking around. There was nothing for miles in either direction. Just this one shop, a tired toilet block, and a bunch of scraggy trees. "Are they all like this?" I asked, stepping down.

Cait jumped down, landing with a thump. "All what?"

"All the towns?"

Cait shook her head. "This isn't a proper town. It's more like a truck stop."

It wasn't even a proper shop. The shelves were half-empty and covered in dust, as if no one had shopped there for years.

"No ice-cream," Cait complained.

"How about biscuits?" I asked, watching the other kids sifting through the biscuit shelf.

Cait nodded and we walked over to join the treasure hunt. But there was hardly anything worth eating. We managed to grab the last packet of some bizarre jammy things.

Cait didn't seem to mind. "I like biscuits more

than ice-creams anyway. Shall we eat them under that tree?"

"Sure."

We headed for the shade of one of the strange, scraggy trees, but we never got that far.

"Miku Mouse! Check this out. It's your cousin!"

I couldn't see Alex, but I sure was fed up with hearing his voice. "It's Miku," I grumbled, to no one in particular. "And check out your own cousin."

I opened the plastic wrapping and offered Cait the first biscuit. They didn't look too bad now the packet was open. "He'd better not be like this all week."

Cait nodded. "He's such an idiot."

But that didn't make him go away. Alex's head popped out from behind the shop. "Serious. It could be your cousin. It's this little Japanese guy, all dressed up like a mushroom. I think he wants to talk." Alex waved us over, then vanished again.

"What a loser," Cait said. "As if we'd fall for that. They'll probably throw water on us."

"Probably." I looked around us at the empty fields, the odd shop. And now a little Japanese guy? "But maybe we should…?"

"Totally," Cait grinned. "Quick. This could be our

only chance to steal their seats."

But I didn't care about the seats. "I was thinking more of…"

Something yelped from behind the shop. Something in trouble. I took off in that direction. Cait scrambled to catch me but missed. "Miku!"

I don't know what I was expecting. Maybe nothing. Another tourist, like us? One of Alex's dumb jokes? But something wasn't right. Pins and needles were prickling in my guts.

I swung around the back of the shop, ready for anything. Instead there was nothing - just stringy weeds and thistles, and Alex and Oscar, jumping around as if they'd seen a ghost. But there was no ghost.

They'd made a fool of me again. I felt my face boil red and I could have kicked myself. I should have listened to Cait.

"What's going on?" I snapped at Alex. "And the name's Miku, so don't even think about saying anything else." I glared at him, willing my eyes to go narrow and cold.

Alex was super-excited. "OK, whatever. But you just missed your cousin. He was here seconds ago. Then he totally disappeared."

Oscar nodded, his cheeks and his eyes bulging.

He must have gulped his snack in one mouthful.

"What do you mean, my cousin?"

"Little guy." Alex held his hand out at chest height, then spun round, searching, as if hunting for a cricket. "Wearing a straw hat, a big round one. Made him look like a mushroom."

Oscar coughed, sending bits of white stuff flying from his mouth, and then he swallowed. "He was here," he spluttered, "dressed in a bed sheet. With weird shoes, like bits of straw all woven into fish nets." His eyes were still bulging.

Alex waved his hands in the air like a TV magician. "And then he disappeared. Poof!"

"And he took that stuff…" Oscar made a face, as if he was trying to spit out the rest of whatever he had been eating. He scanned the area. "And now he's totally gone."

If this was some joke they'd made up, they were doing a good job. The guy sure sounded Japanese. The bed sheet could have been a kimono. The hat was perhaps a sugegasa, the kind worn by travellers and farmers. And the woven shoes sounded like antique zori sandals. But why would they make that stuff up?

"Another stupid story!" Cait grabbed my arm, pulling me towards the bus. "Haven't you got something better to do? We're not that dumb. Come on, Miku."

But I couldn't. I used my toe to prod the white stuff that had exploded from Oscar's mouth.

"What'd you eat that for, anyway?" Alex asked. "It could've been anything."

"I thought it was from the shop," Oscar protested.

"You ate something he gave you?" I tried to stay calm.

"A bit." Oscar looked bashful. "Be rude not to."

"He had this stuff," Alex explained. "On a platter. White and wobbly like jelly." He punched Oscar on one arm. "Told you it wasn't ice-cream."

"Well, that's obvious now." Oscar tried to thump Alex back, but his fist went wide. He rubbed the arm Alex had whacked. "No wonder he disappeared. It tasted disgusting."

"You only just missed him," Alex said, talking to me. "Serious. He just vaporised. Do you think he could be…"

"Serious smearous," Cait interrupted. "Stop making up stories. You're not in kindergarten any more." She took the biscuit packet from me, pulling on my arm.

"Was it tofu?" I asked, ignoring Cait.

"What?"

"This white stuff." I nudged the goop on the ground with my toe.

"Tofu?" Oscar echoed.

"Looks like tofu," Cait agreed, still tugging on my arm. She was getting good at Japanese food - she came round to my place often enough. "But who could think tofu was ice-cream?"

I had to agree. Plus who would accept strange food from a Japanese man in centuries-old costume who just happened to appear in the English countryside with a platter?

The answer was clear: Oscar.

"What?" he protested. "It looked like ice-cream to me."

The bus driver honked his horn. Just two minutes left.

"Come on," said Cait. "Let's leave them to it."

"Serious, Miku." Alex used my real name again. "He was right here, seconds ago. And now..." He looked around, confused.

"Drop it, Alex." Cait grabbed a biscuit and spoke through the crumbs. "We're over it."

But I wasn't over it, not even close.

As Cait pulled me to the bus, I ran through Oscar's options in my head.

Even before we were all back on board, Oscar was beginning to smell. I sneaked a peek at him over my shoulder. He still looked OK, but how would he last a whole week at camp? Of course, he might survive. Baba had told me stories where people did. But most of the time, well, the others weren't so lucky.

"What you looking at?" Oscar asked, and I looked away.

Perhaps it was like Cait had said. Perhaps the boys were just joking and I was over-reacting. But I was worried. Especially when Oscar started to itch.

CHAPTER THREE

Soon I was holding my nose because Oscar's smell was so bad.

His itch had become a rash. Not the red, spotty one you get from touching poison ivy or eating bad sushi. A black, festering one, like something that grows in your shower when you don't clean it for a year. And that's how Oscar was smelling. As if he was beginning to rot.

"Check this out, Alex," he said.

Alex knelt on his seat, peering at Oscar in the seat behind him. "That is so wrong. What is it?"

"Do you mind?" Cait complained. "Some of us are trying to breathe."

"Dude," said Alex. "You need to see a doctor."

But a doctor wouldn't make any difference.

Oscar wasn't that kind of sick. I hunkered down in my seat and tried to think.

Oscar wasn't exactly my best friend in the world, but it didn't make me happy to know he was probably rotting to death. I was pretty sure he'd run stomach-first into a deadly demon: the Tofu Monk, or tōfu-kozō in Japanese. Baba had often warned me about him, a wandering demon known to offer travellers a taste of his wares. His tofu was supposed to look great. Perhaps, if you'd never seen tofu before, it might even look like ice-cream. But if you ate it.... I shuddered.

I had no idea how to cure tōfu-kozō poisoning. Baba hadn't told me that bit. I didn't even know if there was a cure. How long would it take Oscar to rot? How long did we have to find help?

And something else was nagging me. How had the Tofu Monk found us? Had Alex and Oscar happened, accidentally and unluckily, to meet a deadly demon at a random, roadside shop? Or had the demon been expecting us? And what kind of a shop was it, anyway? For the rest of the journey my stomach flipped, as if I'd swallowed a dying fish instead of a biscuit.

About an hour later the bus was still huffing and puffing as it struggled round increasingly tight hairpin bends. The road was getting narrower and the woods were growing thicker. Just when it seemed the bus couldn't go any further, we turned right, trundling down an unpaved road for about a minute before we seemed to tip over the edge of a cliff. The bus's brakes screamed and heaved and some of the kids up the front screamed too.

"Nearly there," announced Mr Lloyd cheerfully. "It's just at the bottom of this hill."

"Hill?" Cait goggled. "This place has to be at the centre of the earth."

The bus skidded and lurched its way down the steepest driveway I'd ever seen. Thick trees rolled by above us and the morning sunlight faded into shadow as we dropped deeper into the valley.

An old green shed appeared as we rounded the corner and Alex stopped drumming to stab his finger at the bus window. "There," he said, so we could all know he'd seen it first. Which he hadn't.

The rest of the campsite was just as disappointing: a river and a few more wooden buildings, huddled together as if they were frightened or cold. They were probably cold. It felt as if the sun never shone this far into the valley. And there were no satellite dishes, no phone lines, no next-door neighbours. A couple of kids rolled their eyes as we filed off the bus.

"Grab your bags and move into the main hall,"

Ms Jackson directed, smiling. "Welcome to camp, everyone."

"Home, sweet home." Cait made a face.

"They better have hot showers," said a girl called Chelsea. She looked over her shoulder at the boys. "And someone needs to tell Oscar about deodorant."

Cait nodded and grimaced. "That guy has a serious problem."

But she didn't know how serious. On the bus I'd tried to explain about the Tofu Monk. Cait had pretended she didn't understand. Probably a good idea. If other kids had been listening we could have caused a mass panic. But as soon as we were alone, I planned to tell Cait everything.

We recovered our bags from a massive pile and then trooped into a hall filled with wooden tables and benches – some sort of dining room, I guessed. It was freezing and there wasn't even a carpet on the floor.

We sat around, staring at a guy Mr Lloyd introduced as Mr James, the camp caretaker. He was dressed in grey trousers, with a baggy T-shirt that had holes in its collar and only just covered his large belly. He didn't look as if he spent much time climbing trees or fording rivers. I guessed he'd be zero help if it came down to hand-to-demon combat.

"Do you think they have TV here?" Cait whispered.

"Welcome to Camp Crossland," Mr James announced. "You've got the place to yourselves all this week. There are no other bookings, so you can spread out. The girls' cabins are along the west side, the boys' cabins are..."

Mr James droned on and I zoned out, thinking of Oscar's rotting rash and the tōfu-kozō demon. When Mr James finished lecturing, Ms Jackson took her turn, explaining how she'd like our behaviour to be exemplary this and make-her-proud that. By the time Mr Lloyd stood up, we were starving.

"I'll make this short," he said. "I've heard great things about the food here. You won't want to be late. Find a bunk, drop your stuff, and we'll see you back here in ten minutes."

We grabbed our bags and ran for the cabins as fast as the 'no running' rule would allow. Our girls' cabin was just as dreary as the dining hall, with cold metal bunks and a colder concrete floor. I was beginning to be pleased I'd brought two pairs of jeans. Maybe I could wear both pairs at once to stay warm.

Cait and I snagged neighbouring bottom bunks, right next to the window so we could at least see the sun, if it ever came out. Cait started arranging her stuff and I checked my case, making sure the lucky charms I'd packed were still there. I waited till the other girls had left, then placed a dried cedar leaf above our cabin door.

"You really think we need that here?" Cait asked, still folding and unfolding her clothes.

"Absolutely." I nodded. The leaf wouldn't protect us against major demons, but it could still help with any smaller demons lurking about. Which reminded me…. "Cait," I began. "About Oscar…"

"Don't worry," she said. "I don't even like him. Who cares if he stinks?" A bell rang from the main hall. "Lunch," Cait said, pushing her case against the wall. "Wonder what it is?"

"I'm not talking about Oscar's smell," I persisted.

Cait looked at me, horrified. "You don't mean…?"

I nodded. "That's exactly what I mean."

"You like Oscar?" Cait said, as if I liked eating spiders.

"No," I protested. "That's not…"

"Oh, totally phew. I thought…"

"No, no, no," I said, as quick as my mouth

would let me. "That's not what I meant."

Cait grinned. "That is a major relief. Because you should see the stuff that's growing on him. He really needs a shower." The bell rang again. "Come on, Miku, we're missing lunch!" She scrambled through the door, leaving me bewildered and blinking like a baby.

We didn't miss lunch, but I kind of wished we had. It was a mountain of ham and salad sandwiches that had to be at least a week old.

Cait rolled her eyes. "I think we're going to starve."

We tried to salvage something edible from our plates, peeling slivers of bread off the concrete crusts and building a skyscraper of brown lettuce in the middle of the table. Mr Lloyd announced the list of activities: hut building, hiking, campfire cooking, (and we even had to eat the cooking). Ms Jackson smelled out Oscar's festering rash and put him straight into the sick bay for a shower and a sleep. I tried again to explain to Cait about the Tofu Monk. I think she tried to understand.

"Poisoned tofu?" she said, flicking more lettuce on to the pile.

"Something like that. Maybe not actual poison. It's different from that. It transforms whoever eats it.

They start to rot."

"So now it's transforming tofu?" She didn't sound convinced. "Don't you think it's just one of Alex's dumb tricks? Maybe there was no tofu guy. Maybe Oscar just needs to shower."

"But you've seen demons. What if they're back, what if they're following us?"

Cait examined her sandwich filling, then shrugged. "Come on, Miku. Even if there was a tofu guy, why would he follow us? I don't think he'd trek halfway across the country just for fun."

I didn't like to point out that a stack of demons had already followed me all the way from Japan. A side trip to the country didn't seem that much further to go. But Cait didn't want to talk demons. She scraped some limp green stuff on to the lettuce pile and frowned at the soggy bread it left behind. "We are seriously going to starve."

After lunch we played camp hockey, dividing into mixed teams and using rolled-up newspapers as hockey sticks. It felt good to be running around, and I even scored a goal against Alex's team, which made me feel a bit better. But not much. Oscar was rotting, Cait was disbelieving. And still my guts were cutting like knives. I stayed on high-alert, waiting for something awful to happen.

And then it did.

Mr James stood up at the front of the class and announced our pre-dinner entertainment.

"Outside," he instructed. "You'll need something warm to wear, and you have five minutes to get it. We meet by the river. No straggling."

The sun was already low, almost ready to dip below the hilltops high above us. Back at the cabins we grabbed a couple of jumpers, and Cait even took her new scarf. By the time we made it to the river, half the class was hovering around an enormous pile of dried wood. The heap was almost as tall as me, stacked with huge logs and then loaded higher with smaller bits. Someone had been collecting firewood for quite a while.

"A bonfire," Cait whispered.

Mr James was crouched at the base of the woodpile, screwing up newspaper and sticking bits into the bottom of the pile. Mr Lloyd was explaining the rules. "Grab a seat, people," he said. "Not too close. This'll be mighty hot once it gets going."

We formed a circle round the woodpile, everyone talking and Cait trying to find a dry spot for her jeans. There was a tiny flare as Mr James lit the newspaper. Soon tendrils of yellow were licking at the wood like the tails of a fox.

In moments the fire was stretching high into the sky, glowing through the quiet of the soft valley light. There was no hint of the musky animal smell that had been haunting me. Instead the air smelled of wood smoke and old leaves and river stones. Maybe we'd be OK. Maybe the knives in my stomach would stop. Maybe Oscar would recover and Cait would understand. If we hadn't been outside in the middle of nowhere, I might almost have relaxed.

"So I'd like you all to give a big thank you to Mr James," Mr Lloyd was saying. "He put a lot of work into this bonfire so that we could enjoy it."

Everyone clapped and hooted until Mr Lloyd held up his hands. "And now," he said, in a low, spooky voice, "over to our host."

A couple of kids giggled, but not me. I was watching, waiting.

Mr James stepped forward. "We have a tradition at Camp Crossland," he began, speaking up as the flames began to roar. "On the first night. Perhaps some of you know it?"

A few kids whispered and giggled, huddling together as the sun dipped even lower. My shoulders grew tight and my nerves began to dance.

"Ghost stories," Mr James announced, and two of the girls shrieked. "Each person tells one story, and one story only. Nothing too violent, no gore. We go clockwise, round the circle."

"Ghost stories!" Cait's eyes glowed in the light of the fire. She grinned at me, but I didn't grin back.

"Keep 'em short," Mr James continued. "You'll all have a turn." He pointed at a kid called Imran, who was staring into the fire. "We'll start with you. Now you've all got five minutes to think of your stories. Get to it."

The class burst into chat but I couldn't hear their words. My head was whirling with the sparks of the fire. I'd heard Mr James's instructions and put two and two together. Trembling, I put up my hand. "Mr James?"

He smiled and walked over. "Yes?"

What could I say? The truth. I gulped and got started. "I don't think we should be doing this."

Mr James looked surprised. "What do you mean?"

I took a deep breath. A couple of the kids fell silent, listening in. "It's just that..."

There was no other way. I had to say it.

"...This could be dangerous," I said, "even deadly. With the fire, and the ghost stories. They used to do it years ago, in Japan. It's a kind of ritual." I hesitated, looking to see if Mr James was still

34

listening. He was, and so was half the class. Talk about embarrassing.

"We call it the Hyaku Monogatari," I struggled on. "It means the Hundred Tales, but there doesn't have to be a hundred. You just need a group of people." I pointed at the kids around me. "This is more than enough." Now everyone was listening. Great.

"Go on," Mr James said. The fire flickered behind him, making odd shadows dance on the sand. I couldn't see his face. Was he actually smiling?

"Well. Like I said, it's a ritual, a way of growing power, so you can call up powerful things. Dangerous things." I waited to be cut off, but no one spoke. "It works just like what we're doing here. Once the group has gathered, you light a fire. You can use smaller fires, like heaps of lanterns, or a big one, like..." I nodded at the bonfire, its flames rippling into the sky. "Like this. Each person tells a story, and as each story is told, one lantern goes out, or the fire gets smaller, like its power is being sapped away." I paused. Every face around the fire was staring at me, their skin flickering in the shadows, their eyes and teeth glowing white. Even Mr Lloyd was sitting silent, watching.

"And then?" Mr James asked, hardly reacting at all.

"And then..." I willed my voice to stay steady. "When the last story is told, the fire goes out. A new evil is created. And a new, powerful demon comes into being."

A log fell from the top of the bonfire, crashing like thunder into the flames and setting off a whirlwind of sparks and smoke. A couple of kids screeched and Alex made some ghost noises.

"Very good," said Mr James. "What was your name?"

"Miku," I said, unsure of his response. Did 'very good' mean we could stop all this and go back up to the hall?

"Miku," Mr James repeated. "Excellent. A great start. Clean, no gore, and very spooky. Thank you. Although next time, please wait till it's your turn."

"It's not a ghost story." I couldn't believe it. "It's a true story. It's not a joke."

"Very good," Mr James chuckled. "But now we must stick to the proper order." He pointed to Imran again. "Remember, keep 'em short and scary."

"But..." I couldn't believe it. He was ignoring my warning.

"Nice one." Cait jabbed me in the ribs. "Spooky. That one of your grandmother's stories?"

"It's real," I insisted. "It's not a story. They really did this. And we're doing it now."

Cait grinned. "We'll just be telling stories, Miku. Most of them won't even be scary."

In a strange way, Cait was right. Most of the stories weren't scary. We went round the circle, listening to each kid tell their tale. There were axe murderers and werewolves, zombies and aliens. All what you'd expect, and none of it true. Some of the kids pretended to be scared, shaking and yelling, that kind of thing. Others tried to spook their friends by making strange noises and throwing rocks into the bushes behind us. But Cait was right. It wasn't the stories that were scary. It was the fire.

It may have been some sort of natural effect. It's probably normal for a bonfire to burn lower with each minute, to gradually dim until there are just embers and a few struggling flames. But what happened with the final story wasn't natural at all.

It was Mr Lloyd's story. Something about this guy who stayed the night in the murderer's section of a wax museum. The guy sits in this chair in the middle of the room, and he starts out convinced that the statues around him are just wax, and that they're no threat at all. But as night draws on, his nerves start to play. He starts to double-guess himself. Was that a blink? A twitch? Are the wax murderers moving? And the next morning he's found, sitting in his chair, as dead as a doornail. The wax statues are still in exactly the same place, so he must've scared himself to death. Or did he? And that's the end.

It wasn't such a great story. Cait even said she'd heard it before. But as soon as Mr Lloyd uttered his final sentence a strange wind whipped up, blowing sand into our eyes and whooshing through the remains of the bonfire. For a second I thought the fire might hold. The embers burned brighter, crackling and glowing so that a final bit of wood burst into flame. But then, as quickly as the wind had arrived, the fire was gone. The embers; the flames; the crackling and glowing. The entire thing was dead. Kaput. And the night it left behind was darker than soot.

Then something howled in the darkness.

And someone screamed.

And Alex made another ghost noise.

And then it was chaos, as if the banks of the river had broken. Everyone ran screaming and laughing away from the river and the bonfire and up to the hall.

But I wasn't laughing.

Oscar's rash was the least of our worries now. The Hyaku Monogatari was no joke. We'd lit our fire, we'd told our stories. And now the fire was out. Something had changed in that instant. Something powerful had been born.

CHAPTER FOUR

At dinner everyone was buzzing from the ghost stories and the spooky wind. Kids sat five or six to a table, picking at the world's most disgusting lasagne and chattering flat-out.

"It was a freak wind. They get them a lot in this valley."

"It was something in the bushes. I heard it crashing around. A badger or pig probably."

"It's a mutant rat, with massive teeth, and it lives in the girls' cabins." This was from Alex. He was sitting at a table of boys, but Oscar was nowhere to be seen. I hoped Oscar was smelling better. Perhaps he would spontaneously recover? Perhaps he'd just eaten some bad ice-cream?

My table was all girls. Cait was telling them extra details about her own story. She'd called it Night of the nukekubi and it was all about how she'd fought a flying-head demon in the school corridors after everyone else was asleep. Nobody believed her, but she didn't seem to mind. "It's not like it actually happened," she said, smiling.

Cait was freaking me out, but just then there was a fuss at the teachers' table. Mr Lloyd did not look happy and Ms Jackson looked positively grim. I guessed it was something to do with Oscar, but I was only half right.

Mr James wiped his mouth with a paper napkin and stood up, scraping his chair. "OK, guys," he said. "Your attention please."

The chatter stopped and kids held their forks in mid-air, watching to see what would come next.

"We've got one extra thing to look out for this week," Mr James said. "It's nothing to worry about really. It's just we've had a call from the farmers next door. They say there's been some strange animal activity in the forest. Badgers, pigs, foxes, stoats.... There's a good chance we'll get a visitor or two at camp, maybe hungry and looking for food. "

"Cool," I heard Chelsea whisper. "Don't you think?"

"Totally," Cait whispered back. "I hope an entire badger family comes to our cabin."

"Remember, guys," continued Mr James. "These are wild animals, not pets. If you see something strange, please report it to me or one of your teachers right away."

I could hardly breathe. Don't get me wrong, wild animals are great, especially when they stay in the wild. But we do a Hyaku Monogatari ritual down at the river, and next thing we get some warning about increased animal activity heading for camp? If my feeling was right, there would be no point in reporting anything to our teachers. Nothing they could do would keep us safe.

Japanese spirits and demons love the animal form, and there are heaps of nasty animal demons: two-tailed undead cats, tigers with the head of a monkey and a snake for a tail, giant rats morphed into human bodies with steel teeth. But these are the obvious ones: if you meet a two-tailed undead cat, you can be pretty sure you're in for trouble.

Worse than these are the Shape Shifters, crafty creatures that change their bodies to suit their mood. And badgers and foxes are renowned for shape shifting. The trouble with a Shape Shifter is that you can't be sure if you're dealing with a friend or an enemy, or even if you're dealing with a Shape Shifter at all. They might start as badgers or foxes, but they can change into beautiful women, or sometimes old men, and Baba once told me of a tanuki who changed into a teapot so he could walk the tightrope! Anything's possible. So you see what I mean. They're unpredictable. And that's when things can get dangerous.

Baba had always taught me to stay on the good side of shape-changing spirits, and in Japan many people do just that. You'll see restaurants with a statue of a tanuki out at the front, to bring fortune and luck. And temples guarded by kitsune, the white foxes, a symbol for the god of rice and prosperity. But Shape Shifters aren't always about fortune and luck and prosperity. Badgers can cheat and steal and kill, foxes can make fire with just a swish of their tails. And they can change their shape in an instant.

If the forest animals were acting up, it would be hard to know who to trust.

"And, guys," Mr James continued. "Oscar Matthews won't be joining us for a couple of days. He isn't feeling well."

I glanced at Cait. She would have to believe me now. First the spooky noises and smells. Then a warning about strange animal activity. And now Oscar....

I put up my hand. "Mr James," I called out.

"Is Oscar going to be OK?"

Mr James looked down his long nose. "He's in the sick bay," he said. "I'm sure he'll be fine."

If you could call being covered in a festering rash 'fine'. I tried to catch Cait's eye, but she wasn't interested. She and Chelsea were mashing their lasagne into soup.

"One more thing." Ms Jackson stood up, wrinkling her nose. "Please don't forget to shower while you're here. You may not shower at home, but you will shower here. For everyone's health and safety. No excuses. Every day."

"That," said Cait, "is disgusting. Who wouldn't shower every day?"

"Oscar Matthews for one," Chelsea giggled. "Didn't you smell him today on the bus?"

The rest of our table sniggered and the talk turned from ghost stories to gossip. The others giggled and whispered while we picked at our dessert – burnt apple pie with watery whipped cream. But I couldn't join in. I kept seeing forest demons flicker before my eyes. What had the Hyaku Monogatari created? I had to get Cait on her own. Surely she would understand.

But I didn't get a chance to talk to Cait until well after dinner, on our way to the showers. The sun was long gone, and yellow lamps lit the concrete paths.

They formed a dotted line of light, like glowing stepping-stones from the hall to the cabins and then on to the shower block. I spoke quickly and kept half an eye on the shadows, watching for glowing eyes.

"Those ghost stories, poor Oscar, the strange animal activity. I think something awful is happening...."

"Oscar just needs to shower," Cait said. "There's nothing wrong with him."

"What about that spooky fire?"

"Come on, Miku. The ghost stories are over."

I shook my head. "It's no story. You've seen demons. You know."

Cait shifted her shower bag from one hand to the other. "Miku, I'm s'posed to be your friend, so I'm going to tell you straight. You don't have to pretend all this is real. It's getting boring, all these demon stories."

I opened my mouth, but nothing came out.

"I'm sorry," Cait continued, "but that's just the way it is. So let's move on, OK?"

I was so gobsmacked I could hear the breeze whistle through my teeth. But what could I say? Nothing.

Then Cait changed the subject, pointing down the path. "Look! Alex has already found a cute critter."

The shower block was shining like an island in the dark. Sure enough, I could see Alex perched on the edge of the concrete, reaching one hand into the shadows.

I launched into a jog, zooming down the path towards Alex and the thing. I could hear Cait's footsteps on my tail, her breathing heavy. "Wait for me!" she cried.

I only slowed down when we drew closer, creeping right up to where Alex was crouching. He was staring at something in the bushes, and the thing's nose was twitching, so it was probably alive.

"See it?" Cait was behind me. She pointed at the bushy black creature. It didn't move. It was hunched low like a ghost in the shadows. "It's a fluffy, forest beastie, no spooky demon here." Her voice was slightly mocking.

"I spotted it," Alex crowed. "I'm the hero. C'mere, buddy." He reached for the creature.

"Don't touch it." I knew I sounded rude, but I could see the thing now. It was incredibly hairy, no bigger than a Chihuahua but fluffier than a puffball. It looked as if it had never had a haircut in its life.

"What's the matter?" Alex boasted. "I'm not afraid of a... thingy. What do you reckon it is?" He didn't wait for an answer, reaching his hand further into the bushes. "C'mere, thingy."

"She's adorable," Cait said. "What's her name?"

"Gotta catch him first. C'mere." Alex stretched his hand into the darkness and the thing bristled.

"Stop it, Alex," I warned. "Don't touch it."

"Why not? C'mon, buddy."

The black thing whimpered, then bared its teeth, backing further into the bushes.

"She's frightened," Cait cooed. "Poor thing. Get her, Alex."

"Don't touch it, Alex. I'm warning you."

Alex looked up. "You're warning me? What's the matter, Miku Mouse? You afraid of cute little beasties?"

"It's not a cute little beastie. I can't tell you more, but trust me, it's not friendly." If I told Alex that demons from the other side of the world were hunting us, half of camp would know in minutes. Then we'd end up with a giant mess of screaming, fainting, freaked-out kids. Not the best way to prepare for a demon uprising.

Alex looked from me to Cait, then back to the hairy thing.

I looked at Cait. She would have to support me now. "Tell him, Cait. You have to tell him. It could be dangerous."

But Cait didn't even blink. "Of course she's friendly. Maybe she's a little lost dog?"

"It's not a dog." I was getting desperate. Part of me wouldn't mind seeing Alex scared to jelly and crying for his mum, but now wasn't the time for games. "Just leave it, Alex. Leave it alone and I'll tell you what it really is."

Alex stopped reaching for the creature and looked across at me. "What do you mean?"

I took a heavy breath. "I mean it's not a forest animal. It's a demon."

Cait sighed. "Not again."

I waited for Alex to freak out or mock me or make a bad joke. But he didn't flinch. He just swivelled on the spot, ignoring the creature to get a better look at me. "What kind of demon?"

"I think it's a keukegen, a small demon, more like a spirit really."

Cait sighed. "Here she goes..."

Alex looked sceptical. "A spirit?"

"Sure. It's Japanese." Now it was my turn to sigh. But Alex didn't tease me. He just listened.

"We have a whole heap of them," I added. "Some are good, some not so good. This one's not so good. If you touch it..."

"What? It bites your hand off and you die?"

49

Cait was mocking. What was up with her?

"Maybe," I snapped. "I just know you shouldn't touch it. It can make you sick. Look what happened to Oscar."

"That was a demon?" Alex gaped.

I nodded. "Oscar needs help, Alex. He needs a cure."

"Oh, please!" Cait exclaimed. "It's her grandmother," she said to Alex. "She told ghost stories and now Miku believes them."

"They're not stories, Cait." I couldn't believe it. "You were there. You've seen them, the nukekubi, the Woman of the Wet. The noppera-bō that looked just like your father."

But Cait just shook her head. "That's just storyland. I'm sorry, Alex. She's been like this for days."

"You've seen a noppera-bō, Cait? You've actually met one?"

"No." Cait shook her head. "I don't think so. Not really...."

"Yes, we did!" I said. "It came right into my house, remember? And it looked like your dad."

Cait looked bewildered.

"Did you see its face?" Alex asked.

Cait said nothing, so I nodded for her.

"Was it empty?"

I nodded again. "No eyes, no mouth, nothing."

Cait just stared, as if she was watching a movie she didn't quite understand.

Alex whistled. "Awesome," he said. "So it's true."

I forgot Cait for a second and looked at Alex. For a class clown he seemed to know a whole lot about noppera-bō.

"I've been reading," he explained, looking down at his hands. "Noppera-bō. The faceless ones. Apparently there's a lot, and they're on the move. They're even in Hawaii now."

But Cait shook her head. "They're only stories, Alex."

"Oscar's rash isn't a story," Alex said. "I've smelt it. It's absolutely real."

I stared at Cait. "You don't remember?" I asked. "Your own dad's face, just melting away?"

For a moment Cait looked confused. Then she stuck out her chin. "No. I don't. Because it never happened."

Alex climbed to his feet. "Let's say it did happen," he said, keeping a steady eye on the keukegen. "I don't s'pose it happened the day the snow came, that time the school flooded?" He didn't wait for an answer. "Because I found this at school, the day after."

He reached up to his throat and pulled a pendant from where it lay hidden under his T-shirt. "It was in the garden, outside a broken window."

I gasped.

"What is it?" Cait asked.

It was white and shiny, and smaller than I remembered, but I recognised it at once.

"It was that teacher's…" Alex guessed, watching my face. "Mrs Okuda. Am I right?"

It was Okuda's all right. A single pearl from the necklace she'd been wearing when her hungry head had detached from her body, when she'd been preparing to eat me and Cait and my little brother Kazu.

"Why are you wearing it?"

"Dunno." Alex looked embarrassed. "Thought it might protect me or something. It worked with the tofu guy. I showed it to him and he didn't even come near." He paused, then looked straight at me, fishing for more information. "Okuda was evil, right?"

What was going on? First Cait seemed to have lost her memory, and now Alex, horrible Miku-Mouse Alex, was talking to me about demons. I waited for him to roll his eyes, to crack a joke.

But his face seemed sincere and his eyes looked truthful. Could it be, for once in his life, Alex was serious? Plus, as a bonus, he hadn't panicked or run off screaming.

"Come on, Miku. I might be able to help. We have to cure Oscar, right? You could at least let me know about that bit."

"Fine, I'll tell you. But you have to leave that thing alone." I nodded my head at the keukegen. It was still cowering under the bushes. "And you're not to tell anyone else."

"Sure." Alex nodded. "I promise."

"Here we go," Cait groaned. "More stories."

"And we should talk somewhere else…" I looked around. "Somewhere safe." Beyond the bright light of the shower block I could see the path lamps and cabin lights shining out like lanterns. It looked almost cheery.

Then, in an instant, everything went black. The lights went out all over camp. I grabbed Cait's arm and froze, listening, still as a stone in the darkness.

Shouting and yelling erupted from behind us, from deep inside the dark shower block, then kids started screaming all over camp.

Chapter Five

Mr James had the lights back on in less than thirty seconds. He'd appeared out of nowhere, shone his torch in a few places and clicked a few switches, and then, just like magic, it was over.

"Probably a short circuit," he said, explaining the power cut with a wave of one hand. "Tripped a fuse maybe. Sorry for the fuss." He seemed totally relaxed, as if he was having a cup of tea or reading the newspaper. As if his camp was regularly plunged into complete and utter darkness.

Mr Lloyd looked anything but relaxed. He had arrived from the teachers' cabin at full speed, and was still trying to catch his breath. And Ms Jackson had her hands full with hysterical kids. "A power cut is no excuse not to shower," she was saying. "You'd shower at home so you will please shower here as well."

I looked around for the keukegen, but the hairy demon had disappeared.

"I'm not going in there, no way." Chelsea shook her head and clung to one of her trembling pals. "I heard something move."

Where had the demon gone? And why had it shown up in the first place?

"It's OK," Ms Jackson reasoned. "It was a technical fault, that's all."

"But there was something in there," Chelsea moaned. "I swear I heard it move."

"What if it's a mouse?" wailed someone else. "Or a nest of mice? Big mice."

Someone made a ghost noise and a couple of the kids started crying. "What if it's a murderer?"

Ms Jackson looked at Mr Lloyd and he shrugged. She had to give in. "Fine. OK. Those who prefer to shower tomorrow may do so, this one time only. Just don't forget to wash properly. There's only room for one in the sick bay."

Chelsea and the rest of the class scampered, unwashed and jittery, back to their cabins. I watched them go and shivered, but not from the cold. Whatever had caused that blackout, it wasn't a technical fault.

What was I going to do? I couldn't protect my class from all the demons that might be lurking, especially if Cait wasn't going to help. I needed back-up. I'd have to find Ms Jackson, explain everything. We had to go home.

"Ouch," Cait complained. "You're hurting me."

"Sorry," I mumbled, releasing my grip on her arm.

"Come on, Miku, you heard. We can shower tomorrow."

"Just a sec." I looked round. The keukegen wasn't the only thing to have disappeared. "Where's Alex?"

Cait shrugged. "Don't know, don't care. It was probably him in there, making all that noise in the first place."

I stared at her. "But he was out here with us. Remember?"

Cait stared at me. "Whatever."

"Pssst." A call came from inside the shower block, making me jump. Alex poked his head round the door. "In here," he whispered. "I think I've found something."

"Alex, wait…" But he had gone back into the shower block.

"Troublemaker," Cait sniffed. "Come on, let's get back to where it's warm."

She started walking back up to our cabin and I looked from her to Alex as if it was a tennis match. I couldn't leave Alex in there alone, but I couldn't leave Cait by herself either – not when she was acting so strange. "Come on." I dragged her in Alex's direction, expecting a complaint. Instead she just rolled her eyes and came with me. "I just have to check on something," I bluffed.

We went into the shower block. Alex wasn't in the corridor that separated the boys' from the girls', so we had to choose one block to search first. It didn't feel right to go into the boys' showers first. Plus Alex was just as likely to be in the girls' showers, waiting to spook the next poor girl to walk in.

We turned right and crept into the girls' shower room. Our footsteps echoed as if we were deep underground and I could hear water plink-plonking from somewhere far away. The whole place seemed empty. Cubicles lined one wall; basins and mirrors lined the other. I watched our reflections as we crept forward, checking to make sure they crept forward with us.

Cait grinned at me in the mirror. "Spooky, huh?" she said, as if she was actually enjoying it.

We searched each cubicle, half-expecting Alex,

half-expecting the keukegen or one of his pals. But every shower was empty.

"What do you think of my hair like this?" Cait asked, holding her curls in experimental pigtails, and surveying herself in the mirror.

"Cute," I admitted, wondering how she could be so calm. I scanned the room again, searching ceiling corners, behind doors. If Alex wasn't in here, then...

Something hissed at us from behind. Alex's head appeared again. "Over here." He beckoned towards the front door. "I think I've found it."

"Alex, wait..." But again he was gone.

"Really cute?" Cait asked, double-checking her pigtails.

I felt as if I was babysitting two lots of Kazu on his most mischievous day. "Come on, Cait, quick."

We stole back across the room in time to see Alex disappearing into the boys' shower room.

"Are you sure?" Cait looked uneasy. "I mean, we don't know what's in there, do we? It could be anything."

She was finally being serious. "You mean like demons?"

She shook her head. "I mean like boys' stuff. Their showers and toilets and stuff. Who knows what they have in there. I don't want to know."

Alex's head appeared round the corner again. It seemed to have a life of its own and I shuddered, remembering Mrs Okuda's head as it zoomed separately from her body. Thankfully, Alex's head was still well attached.

"In here," he mouthed, holding a single finger to his mouth. "Shhhh."

We tiptoed closer, and saw he was standing right at the entrance to the boys' shower room. There was a large cupboard in the place where the girls' showers had extra toilet cubicles, and Alex was standing right outside its slim wooden door. The door was firmly shut, and creamy paint was peeling away from the corners. The handle looked as if it would fall right off if you turned it. The cleaning cupboard?

Something clinked from behind the door.

"Alex…" I furrowed my brow, trying to look as strict and stern as Mr Lloyd did on the rare occasions that Alex actually listened to him.

Alex just grinned and held his finger to his lips. "Shhhh."

Another something tinkled from behind the door. Then there was a scrabbling sound.

"It's moving," Cait breathed. "Is it the furball?"

"Let's get it," Alex mouthed, and Cait nodded.

"Guys…" I whispered.

Cait started counting on her fingers. One.

"Cait," I tried again. "This is..."

Cait held two fingers up.

"...not a..."

Cait held up three fingers and Alex hurled the door open. Inside, something shrieked and something metal clattered to the floor, crashing like symbols.

"...game," I finished lamely.

Light from the corridor streamed into the cupboard, revealing a mess of mops and buckets. Further back it was still as dark and deep as the interior of a well. I glimpsed a shadow, too large to be be the keukegen, scooting sideways. Then everything went still. I opened my mouth to warn Cait and Alex, but they were already inside.

"It's in here," Cait said. "I saw it move."

Great. So *now* she believed in demons?

"I saw it too, back there." Alex pointed with one hand and held on to Okuda's pearl with the other.

I followed his pointing finger and could just make out an animal shape, hovering in the darkness.

Cait fumbled at the wall and the entire cupboard exploded into light. A red creature scrambled up and over and across the shelves. Buckets clattered, mops toppled, boxes fell to the floor. Then everything went quiet.

"What do we do now?" Cait whispered.

I wished she'd thought about that earlier. I edged inside the cupboard, scanning the mess for signs of life. There. I spotted something strange, sticking out from behind some old paint tins. It looked like an elbow. Was it an arm? The skin was rust-red and smooth, like that of a snake or a fish. It didn't look good.

"Miku." Cait reached for me. "What is it?"

I had no idea.

A shy eye appeared over the top of a paint lid, and the cans of paint seemed to speak. "Are you hers?" The creature pointed a webbed finger at Alex. "The nukekubi. Is she here?"

Alex gaped. Cait moved to stand behind him.

"The pendant," the creature said, its voice scrabbling like pebbles in a stream. "Are you hers?"

I turned to look. Alex's pendant was still hanging from his neck, the pearl glowing in the white light of the cupboard.

"No," I answered, trying to stay calm. The creature was still hidden behind paint cans, but it sounded more petrified than dangerous. "I mean yes. She's not here, but that's her pearl. Used to be."

The thing moved, revealing a hairy head and long, hairy tongue that darted in and out. The creature was smaller than I'd expected. And it looked frightened. "Used to be?"

I took a risk and told it the truth. "The nukekubi has gone. We crushed her. Well, the Woman of the Wet did anyway."

"The nure-onna?" it asked. It edged forward, licking one eye.

It seemed to know the Woman of the Wet, our half-snake half-woman demon-killing friend. "Yes." I swallowed. "And you are?"

"Really gone?" it asked.

"Really gone. That pearl is all that's left...."

The thing did a noisy jig on the paint shelf and then leapt to the floor. In the light I could see its entire body. It was no bigger than Kazu, perched on all fours and covered in rust-red frog skin.

Cait gasped and Alex took a quick step backwards, nearly tripping over her. But I didn't move. The creature's tiny face was creased into what I guessed was a grin, and I think the dancing meant it was happy. "Have you come to set me free?" it asked.

"Free?"

The thing cantered on the spot. "Free. Free." Then it stopped to lick one arm. Except for the webbing between its fingers, its hands seemed quite ordinary, connected to strong arms and each with five fingers and five fingernails, all where you'd expect them. But its feet were something else altogether. I tried not to stare.

"What are you?" Cait whispered.

The thing didn't answer. Instead it flushed redder and began licking its other arm.

"Are you with that keukegen?" Alex asked, and the red thing looked up.

"Are *you*?" it asked. "He's…" The creature broke off, intent on licking one long, powerful leg.

I stared at its feet. They had one toe each and looked more like sharpened hooves.

"My pet," it continued, still licking. "He is my pet and he's run off." The creature tutted like Mum when she looks at my calligraphy. "Have you seen him?"

"He was outside," Alex said. "Disappeared when the lights went out. Hey, was it you who caused that commotion earlier? With the lights? The girls were screaming. It was awesome."

"Awesome?" The thing stopped licking and looked up.

"Yeah. Very. Could you show me how to do it sometime?"

"Awesome. Awesome." The thing hopped on the spot like an enormous frog. "I'm very awesome," it said, dabbling one hand through a mop of

black hair. "Very. And clean. I like to be clean."
It studied each of us in turn. "Do you keep clean?"

Then I realised, and I blurted it out. "You're a
Filth Licker."

Mum wasn't big into demons, but even she
believed in aka-na-me, the Filth Lickers. Or at least
she'd threatened me with them plenty of times.
She'd use them to try and scare me into cleaning
the shower, but I'd always figured it was easier
to bar the front door with cedar leaves than scrub
the bathroom.

Plus Baba always said they were harmless. During
the day they hid in the shadows, and at night they
crept out to eat slime and mould from the walls of
dirty bathrooms. Disgusting, but useful.

"Whoah, Miku. That's pretty harsh," said Alex.
"You could at least be friendly."

The thing thumped its hoofed toe on the ground,
twitching like a nude rabbit, but said nothing. Then it
bent to lick its other leg.

But it was true. 'Aka' meant 'filth' and 'na-me'
was 'lick'. There wasn't much I could do to change
that.

"It can also mean dirt," the Filth Licker said,
almost reading my mind. "Or grime. Or earwax.
And I also lick slime. And mould." He looked up.

"It's not so bad. Someone's got to keep this shower block clean."

"You live here?" Cait wrinkled her nose.

"I do now," it said, looking at the ground.

"With the keukegen?"

"I guess so." It licked one single-toed foot.

"Noticed anything weird lately?" I asked, probing for information. "Tofu sellers? Monks? Any strange forest activity?" Filth Lickers weren't anywhere near being dangerous, so if this one wanted to talk, it might as well say something useful. Aka-na-me had relatives all over the place: Lamp Lickers. Ceiling Lickers. Face Lickers. And we all know how relatives like to talk. Baba said Filth Lickers got to hear a lot of news.

"Activity?" it asked, patting its woolly hair with webbed fingers.

"Yes. Anything about Shape Shifters? Or badgers? Maybe a fox?"

It thumped one foot on the floor and swung its head around. "*Osoroshii*," it said, shivering. "Awful. They're everywhere."

"Shape Shifters?" I asked.

"They're hungry," it said, tongue darting in and out of its mouth. "Always hungry. And I cannot see them in the dark. What chance would I have?" It licked one arm furiously, then looked up,

66

lip quivering. "I'd be snapped up. In one mouthful. A Shape Shifter's dinner. I am trapped," he wailed, mouth working in circles, chewing at the air. "I cannot ever leave."

Cait stood agog at the outburst. Alex looked shocked, polishing his pearl with one hand.

"Leave where?" I prompted.

The creature looked round, suddenly furtive. "There is a new demon rising," it whispered. "A super-demon, growing stronger. You must get to the farm. You must face it, before it grows too great."

"What kind of demon?" My heart was thumping in my ears. I'd been right. The Hyaku Monogatari had created another evil. "Which farm?"

"Over the hill," the demon gestured. "Across the forest. And you must go tonight. Tomorrow will be too late."

Something shuffled from the back of the shed and the keukegen tumbled in from the shadows, its puffball hair filled with dirt and leaves.

It sat in the corner and stared, and the Filth Licker wouldn't breathe another word.

CHAPTER SIX

Alex begged the Filth Licker to come with us, but the little red demon wouldn't so much as peep outside the door of his cupboard. Instead he cowered on the floor, muttering nonsense about foxes and badgers, and licking his shiny limbs.

And the fur-ball keukegen just sat there, blinking in its dark, damp corner.

"We have to leave them behind," I insisted. "And I'm leaving now, tonight."

I'd been right, something had been brewing, and now the worst had happened. Whatever demon the Hyaku Monogatari had created, its power was growing, and from the way the Filth Licker was quaking on his one-clawed feet, it wasn't going to be pleasant.

We have a saying in Japanese, that you must enter the tiger's cave if you want to catch its cubs. I wasn't sure if the thing we were hunting was still a cub or already a tiger, but it wasn't going to be friendly. And waiting would only help it grow stronger.

At first I tried to go alone. I figured these demons were my responsibility and I'd already put my whole class at risk by coming to camp. Oscar could be just the first to pay the price for my foolishness.

"I'll be fine," I bluffed. "Nothing I can't handle. Plus, it's not safe for you to come." At least that bit was true.

"Not a chance." Cait squeezed me on the shoulder. "You were right about the demons, I've seen the Filth Licker now, and the fur-ball. I'll help you fight this new one."

"Thanks," I stammered, grateful and worried at the same time. Could I really count on Cait? She wasn't herself. She seemed to change her opinion like the wind changed direction.

"I'm absolutely coming, Miku," Cait said, perhaps sensing my confusion. "Don't even think about leaving me behind."

And I hadn't been sure about including Alex in our demon-hunting team, but I could either trek through the dark forest with only Cait and her erratic memory.

Or go with Cait and the school's most annoying class clown. Neither option was great.

But in the end Alex wouldn't be left behind. "I'm coming too," he insisted. "I know too much." He fingered Okuda's pearl. "Plus I've got to help Oscar."

I didn't like to tell him Oscar's troubles were only the beginning. Our whole class was in danger, and there wasn't time to get help or go home. We had to stop this super-demon now, before it grew stronger.

"What's that thing round your neck?" Cait asked, looking at Alex's pearl with genuine confusion. "Some girl's necklace?"

So that sealed it. Cait was getting worse. At least Alex would be useful as her babysitter, if nothing else. "You don't remember the nukekubi?" I asked. "Mrs Okuda and her flying head?"

Cait looked at me as if I was crazy.

"She was in your story," I prompted, "from the bonfire."

"I made that up," Cait said. "That stuff's not real. What's going on?"

I cringed. "We've got to find out. Let's get a move on. We've got to get to this farm."

"Sweet," Alex crowed. "Way to go, Miku Mouse." He dropped into a commando pose. "Move out,

70

team," he grunted. I glared at him and he scooted away.

We left the Filth Licker and the keukegen in the cleaning cupboard and ran back to the cabins, watching every shadow as we passed. Inside our cabin, Cait and I grabbed torches and stuffed our sleeping bags with old clothes and pillows, hoping it might look as if we were asleep.

With everything ready, we waited for Alex outside, listening to the rest of our class laughing and talking down at the dining hall. They were probably sipping hot chocolate and eating custard creams. Part of me wanted to join them, but instead I zipped up my jacket.

"You think we'll be OK?" Cait whispered, pulling her scarf a little tighter. "You checked your torch batteries?"

I nodded, not sure which question I was answering. Alex was taking forever and the cold was creeping into my bones. "It'll be warmer once we start walking," I whispered.

"And I thought girls took a long time to get ready," Cait said, rolling her eyes.

By the time Alex appeared I was freezing. "Sorry I'm late," he said. "I couldn't find my beanie." He pulled a scruffy woollen hat over his head.

"It's freezing out here."

"We know," I said. "If you're ready?"

Alex nodded, waving his hand with a flourish.

And that was that. We just started walking away from the lamplight, away from the campsite, into the forest. No one yelled or tried to stop us. No demon badgers or steel-toothed rats stood in our way. With every step my heart and blood grew warmer. It was way easier than I'd thought. Too easy.

We followed an old dirt trail between the gurgling river and the woods, keeping our torches off to save batteries. The moon was just a sliver, but it was still enough to see. I guess we walked for about an hour, until there was no real track and the river shrank away to nothing. Then I had to concentrate on where we were going, but it was always up, up, and out of the valley. Dark trees closed in around us, branches loomed and undergrowth scratched at our jeans.

Once we left the babbling of the river, the only sound was our puffing and the swish of our clothes, as if the forest was waiting, holding its breath. Then we began to hear the hooting of owls and the murmur of the wind through the trees. Ahead of us, leaves crackled and night creatures snuffled, probably real badgers or rats or angry hedgehogs. But there was no strange forest activity, no supernatural spirits.

I focused on building a rhythm with my steps and my breathing. Behind me I could hear Cait panting louder with every step. Alex was silent: he seemed to be doing just fine. And now that we were moving, I felt calmer. The only problem was, I didn't know where we were going. I just knew we needed to get to the farm, and that meant climbing out of this valley.

I breathed in the wet, rich, leafy air. There was no sign of the smell that had been haunting me. Everything seemed peaceful, normal, fine. Maybe we'd been wrong to rush off. Had I over-reacted? These smells reminded me of forests in Japan, back in the time when things had been safe.

When Baba was still young enough to walk with a single stick, she and I had wandered Kawanishi's trails almost every weekend. We'd follow rivers into secret gorges, trek to tiny mountain shrines, pay our respects to the gods who protected the forest and the creatures who lived in it. I peered through the night, straining to spot any creatures that might be watching us. And I wished Baba could be with us now. She'd know the right thing to do.

In Japan, our family had been protected. Our house had been haunted by our zashiki-warashi, a house ghost we called Zashiko. She'd looked after my family for generations. She kept the other demons away. And all the time Zashiko was looking out for us, Baba had been there in the background, looking out for Zashiko. Always kind. Always ready. And we'd never had demon trouble, not in all the years she'd been alive. But after Baba died we'd moved to England, and that was when our demon troubles started.

"Get lost!" A human voice interrupted my thoughts, echoing through the forest. It belonged to Cait.

I stopped climbing and turned round, glad of the rest. "What's going on?"

"My legs," Cait puffed, kicking and scratching at nothing in the darkness. "There's something curling round my legs. I can feel it."

I looked, but saw nothing, just dark undergrowth and the black path.

"Get off," she complained, still kicking.

I looked again. Was she imagining things? Or maybe she just wanted a break from the climb. "You'll be fine," I said, still panting myself, and I turned to climb again.

But in seconds I felt something curling round my own legs, like the tail of a cat or a wisp of soft cotton. I stopped and looked down. There was nothing.

I started walking and could feel it again, dragging round my ankles and tangling my limbs. "It's a trick," I guessed. "A forest sprite. We just have to ignore it." Whatever was waiting for us at the farm had recruited a support crew.

"Are you sure?" Cait asked, still whacking at her legs.

"Certain," I said bravely. "It's quite normal. These sprites will all be out tonight, trying to stop us." I swallowed and kept climbing, trying to ignore the strange tugging at my legs.

Alex slapped at his legs a couple of times but ploughed on. But Cait could hardly move. She kept slapping at her ankles and kicking at the darkness. "Rubbish. Now I've broken a lace."

Cait was so slow it took ages to get anywhere. It wasn't just the sprites causing trouble. The forest was changing. There was nothing friendly about these hills any more. Above us the trees grew more twisted and sinister with every step. Their canopies strangled the light, leaving narrow shafts that stretched like bony fingers to the ground. And with every step the climb seemed to get steeper, as if the valley was trying to swallow us back down.

When at last the ground levelled off, I nearly cheered. I felt as if I'd won the school cross-country.

We came out into a clearing, staring across the blackness of the night. I could just see the flicker of camp lights, way behind us in the valley.

"We made it," Alex announced. He didn't even seem puffed.

"You did well," I said grudgingly.

"Climbing is no worries for a champion like me," Alex said, punching his chest. "I could go on like this for ever. My powers are limitless."

Idiot, I thought, wondering how much of this we'd have to put up with. We watched the lights for a minute longer, so Cait and I could catch our breath.

"Do you think Oscar will be OK?" Alex asked suddenly. "I mean, he'll be all right, right?"

I studied him for a second. Maybe he wasn't such an idiot after all. I mean, he was brave enough to have come with us. And he did seem to care about his friend. "I'm not sure about Oscar," I said. "Not yet. We need to find out more."

"What kind of more?"

We spotted a path that led away from the valley, deeper into the woods. And so I started walking and talking. I didn't know quite where we were going, but it felt good to be moving, and besides, why wouldn't there be a path leading to the farm? Mr James probably went there all the time, for cups of tea and to chat with the farmers about the weather and stuff.

As we trekked, I told Alex all I knew about Oscar and the tōfu-kozō demon. Then I started on other stuff, from the last time Cait and I had faced the demons. I told him about my brother's sudden sickness, the snow that had cancelled school and the o-kubi, the giant face Cait had spotted hanging in the sky.

"Are you sure this really happened?" Cait interrupted, confused. "I mean, I saw that Filth Licker thing just an hour ago, so I know he's real, but I don't remember all this other stuff."

I just nodded and kept talking. We'd have to deal with Cait's memory malfunction later.

When I got to the bit about the nukekubi demon, Alex shivered. "Her head could fly," I explained.

"You mean detach and fly around?" he asked, one hand at his neck.

"Uh-huh." I was whispering now, my words drifting through the dark trees with their ebony shadows. In a strange way I was enjoying myself, talking up our big adventures. "The pearl you're wearing came from her necklace. She wore it to hide the bit that stitched her head to the rest of her body."

"Whoah." Alex looked around, peering into the darkness. "So these demons could be anywhere?

And anyone?"

"Ouch." Cait slapped at her ankles. "This keeps getting harder, Miku. Now I feel like we're moving through sand."

"Yeah," I said. "They could be anywhere. And anyone."

Then it struck me, like a thunderclap from a clear sky. What if…?

Was the person behind me even Cait? Why couldn't a noppera-bō pretend to be Cait, just like it had pretended to be her dad?

But no. She couldn't be. I thought back to the shower block, our reflections in the mirror. Cait's reflection had been totally normal, no eggshell face, all her features exactly where they should be. So she couldn't be a noppera-bō. She had to be Cait.

Or did she? Something new jolted my brain. What if this wasn't Cait. What if it was a Shape Shifter pretending to be Cait, but actually in league with the super-demon we were hunting? A badger or a fox could have abducted the real Cait and replaced her body, and now this could be a Shape Shifter acting in her place. That would explain her strange behaviour. The memory loss. And it would mean we were walking into battle with an enemy spy at our side. What a cunning plan, a perfect revenge.

"Hey, Cait," I said carefully. "There's a path here now. You want to go first?"

Slowly, cautiously, I dropped my pace, letting Cait take the lead. I stopped talking and started listening, and I was watching all the time. Cait pulled ahead, her shoulders heaving as she breathed.

I strained my eyes and ears, and focused on Cait. Was she unusual in any way? Was there any sign of supernatural powers?

Something hissed at me from behind, right inside my ear. I jumped and spun round. It was Alex.

"What?" I glared at him.

"I said *red hair*," he whispered. "Cait's got it. Oni have red hair too."

I kept walking. "What do you know about oni?"

"I know they're ogres," he hissed. "Like Shrek, but with red hair."

"Shrek is make-believe," I said. "And Cait's hair's not red. It's brown. She's not an oni."

"Well, something's up," Alex whispered. "Her brain's gone coo-coo. She can't remember stuff. If she's not an oni, then what is she?"

"Not now. We'll deal with Cait later. We're getting too close to the farm."

But that was a lie. The truth was, I didn't know where the farm was, and I didn't know what to do about Cait. Plus, I was kicking myself. All the good-luck charms I'd so carefully packed in my case were back at camp, still carefully packed in my case. And we were too deep in the woods to turn back. All we could do was go forward. At least Alex was turning out to be useful. He'd probably studied manga more than he'd studied maths.

We were ploughing through a cold part of the woods now, with the trees grown too tall and too dense to let much light trickle through. The path was faint and what little light there was seemed to swim before us, blurring into a mist that shrouded the trees. I squinted at the darkness, as if I was wearing Baba's coke bottle glasses. I could still make out Cait, up ahead and breathing heavily. Wisps of her breath shone white in the cold.

"Ouch." She slapped at her neck. "Ow-ww." She stopped walking and grabbed down the back of her shirt, itching and smacking.

"What now?" Alex moaned.

"Something bit me." She slapped at the side of her head. "A mosquito maybe. Get away!" She slapped her neck and then her own face. "Get lost!"

I cringed. She was acting like a child. Could she really be a Shape Shifter? "You need to relax," I said. "They feed on fear."

She scrabbled at her face, then held something invisible up to her eye. "No, wait. It's... sand."

"Sand bit you?" Alex scoffed.

"Not now, Alex," I snapped.

"Something's dropping sand on me," Cait rambled, glaring at the twisted branches above us. "Like rain. It's raining sand." She slapped at her neck again. "It's everywhere. Miku, help me."

I grabbed her by the shoulders. "You have to relax. They're sprites, they're just trying to scare you."

Cait writhed in my grip, clawing at her hair and scratching down the back of her shirt. "They're attacking me." She whirled around, flailing her fists. "Help! Get away!"

I let her go. "Cait, you've got to chill out. Be calm and they'll leave you alone."

"She's mental." Alex shrugged.

Then Cait's voice rang out again, clear as a bell at midnight. "Help! Get away!" Her words sounded from deep inside the foggy forest, but Cait was right by my side. At once she looked up, eyes wide with horror.

"That wasn't me," she whispered. "I didn't say that."

Her voice echoed again, swirling through the mist between the trees. "I didn't say that. That wasn't me."

I looked at the Cait at my side and then searched for the Cait in the haze. Was the real Cait somewhere out there, needing my help?

"What's going on?" Cait asked, panicking. She slapped at her legs, whirling like a firework. "What is it?"

"What is it?" the forest echoed. "What's going on?"

"Miku!" Cait cried.

"Miku!" the forest echoed.

I stared into the trees but there was nothing. If the real Cait was out there, she'd be yelling something else now, something useful. The echoes had to be just forest sprites, messing with our ears. I looked at the Cait by my side. She was cringing and afraid, her eyes wide. But could we trust her? She'd been acting so strange. But I made up my mind. No Shape Shifter could be this afraid of forest sprites.

"They're sprites," I said, keeping my voice calm. "Probably not evil. They're just silly tricksters. We're perfectly safe in the forest." I hoped I sounded confident. And I hoped I'd made the right decision. When I looked into Cait's eyes she was calm for a second. She held my gaze as we waited, still as grave markers, for the forest to echo my words.

Nothing came.

"It's only me," Cait wailed, panicking again. "They're coming especially for me."

"It's only me!" Her words echoed through the mist. "They're coming especially for me!"

"Shhh." This time it was Alex who spoke. His eyes were wide. "Listen. Something really is coming."

CHAPTER SEVEN

The three of us stood, ears cocked like dogs.

Above us the mist whistled through the trees, coiling into eddies and fogs. At first I couldn't hear anything. I figured it was just another of Alex's dumb jokes. Then I heard tree trunks cracking and crashing from somewhere behind us.

Something was coming, just as Alex had said. Something big.

I stared into the woods we'd just come through, stretching my eyes so wide they burned with the cold, then squashing them so tight I could barely see. Nothing.

Something Baba had told me floated to the top of my head. "Stand aside," I whispered, herding Cait and Alex with my hands. "To the side of the path."

"What's going on?" Alex protested.

"Just do it."

The three of us scurried to the side of the path and huddled under a tree, so close its brushes caught at our necks and legs. I could hear the thing coming closer.

"What's this about? We should be running," Alex hissed.

"We might be blocking its way," I whispered, hoping my hunch was correct. I took a deep breath. And then I called out, filling the forest with my words. *"Betobeto-san, saki e okoshi."*

I held my breath, listening to the crashing of the thing getting closer.

"What was that?" Cait hissed.

"I asked it to go ahead," I whispered.

"What'd you do that for?" Alex asked.

"It's called being polite."

Alex shrugged. "Whatever makes you happy. We could be dying here."

"Shhhh."

We huddled at the side of the path, hoping and breathing and staring until our eyelids stuck to our eyes. If I was right, the footsteps belonged to a forest phantom, Betobeto-san, a demon that feasted on sound. It was harmless once you said the right words.

I winced as the crashing grew louder. The thing hadn't stopped. In fact it was getting closer. I felt as if I could hear each twig snap and each leaf rustle as the thing pushed through the woods, heading straight for us. This wasn't a forest phantom. This was something bigger, and much worse.

"Isn't the moon pretty," Cait whispered.

"Shhh," I warned her, eyes wild.

Cait stood up straight and skipped into the middle of the path. "What a lovely night," she said, stopping to hold a leaf in one hand. "It's so nice to go for a walk."

"Come back," I hissed. And my nose twitched. What was that smell?

"Cait," Alex whispered, his voice urgent. "It's coming. The demon..."

"Oh, not you too." Cait frowned, dropping her leaf. "You know they're not real. It's all make-believe."

Alex's jaw dropped. "What? What about earlier..?"

Before he could finish, something burst into view on the path ahead.

My nostrils flooded and the back of my throat seized up. I gagged, trying to breathe. It was that smell, the animal smell that had been haunting me for weeks. It was stronger than ever before and it reeked of musty, unwashed bodies.

"Oh," said Cait. "It's the pretty monkey."

A giant monkey-thing stood, hackles raised, in the centre of the path. It was black with a flat nose and wild, glowing eyes. It stood on its two hind legs and it was huge, miles taller even than Alex.

Cait froze, stuck in the centre of the path.

"We're heading to the farm," the creature said, its voice rumbling like a bear's. "We're tracking a super-demon."

It glared at us and bared a set of jagged, white teeth. When it took a step forward the stench grew even stronger. I wanted to scream, but the acrid smell was raking the back of my throat.

"When we find it," the thing said, "we're going to defeat it. You'll never stop us."

"I think it's friendly," Alex murmured. "I'm going to try talking."

I opened my mouth, but nothing came out.

Alex stepped on to the path beside Cait. "That's awesome," he said. "We're hunting a super-demon too. Perhaps we could go together. You look a handy guy to have on our side."

The creature ignored him. "I liked the keukegen," it continued, "but we're not to touch it, Miku said."

"Yeah, well I liked it too." Alex grinned.

"But Miku's the boss when it comes to demons, right, Miku?" He turned to look at me.

I could only stare back. My eyes were stinging and my breath seemed cemented in my lungs.

"That Filth Licker was funny," the monkey creature continued. "I was scared at first, but he seemed harmless in the end." It kept talking, and Alex kept listening.

"I liked him too," Alex said. "So, I'm Alex. Who're you?"

The demon ignored him. "I'm not sure about the tōfu-kozō. I didn't see him, but Miku believes."

Something was wrong. Cait hadn't moved from where she was standing in the centre of the path. Her eyes had glazed over, as if she was suddenly too exhausted even to blink. Drool escaped from one corner of her mouth.

"I saw him," Alex continued chattily. "He was real all right. So what was your name again?"

"I'm really enjoying camp," the demon said. "The ghost stories were amazing and I'm looking forward to campfire cooking. That sounds fun."

Alex looked across at me. "Maybe you'd better try," he whispered. "I'm not getting anywhere."

I squeezed out one word. "Careful." I forced myself to think beyond the paralysing stench.

There had to be a way out of this mess.

"It's a pity Oscar is so sick," the creature continued, scratching its chest with one hairy paw. "I kind of like him. But not as much as Alex." It looked up, staring. "I really like Alex. He's funny and cute and his fringe is so floppy. I just want to stroke it. And he's so brave. He knows about Japanese demons. Even Miku was impressed."

Alex's eyes grew wide. He took a step back from the monkey-monster and his face boiled in the moonlight. I looked at his fringe for the first time. It *was* quite floppy.

I checked on Cait. She was slouched over and drooling heavily, her eyes as dry and lifeless as rock.

Alex took another step back, narrowly missing Cait. He took one look at our motionless, dribbling friend, and turned to me. "What's going on?"

I shook my head and then focused. "Not sure."

We stared at the creature. It bared its teeth at us. And a big gob of slobber fell from Cait's mouth.

"Maybe it's hypnosis," I guessed, forcing my tongue to speak. "Or mind-reading."

"Like it's skimming her thoughts?" Alex asked. "Are you sure?"

"Or telepathy." My brain was fizzing.

"What do we do?"

"I'm frightened," the thing said. "But we've got to keep going." It drew itself up to full height and beat at its chest, sending stink surges rolling through the air. I gagged again.

Alex seemed immune to the smell. "She could fight it," he suggested. He turned to Cait, then spoke to the demon instead. "Fight it, Cait," he urged. "Try to resist it."

The creature's hackles rippled and it stared at us. Cait gave a little moan and slumped to her knees, dribbling from her chin. The animal smell was hot and thick and I felt myself starting to choke. Then the creature's face twisted into a smirk. Was it smiling?

"I don't like lasagne," it said, speaking faster. "That was the worst I've ever tasted. Maybe I'll sit next to Alex next time. Alex doesn't smell. He's so handsome. And strong."

Words were tumbling like grains of rice from its mouth and still it didn't stop. "Alex was only four seats away from me at the bonfire," it said, "and just the next-door table for dinner. We were so close on the bus I could have reached out and touched him. I wonder if he noticed my new jeans."

Alex turned to Cait. Slobber was hanging from her chin and her eyes were rolled back in her head. I'm pretty sure he wasn't noticing her jeans.

"I don't think it's working," he said.

Cait fell to her knees on the forest floor and the creature bared its teeth once again. "I've broken my lace," it said, spitting Cait's words like bullets. "Now I'm getting a blister. Do you think Alex noticed my haircut? Where's the pretty monkey?"

With each word the demon stood taller.

"Maybe she has to stop," I said. "Maybe every thought is giving this creature strength. She has to stop thinking."

"Ms Jackson's outfit was awful. We're lucky the stars are so bright. Did I pack a raincoat? Isn't Alex great?"

"Stop thinking..." Alex echoed. "How do you do that?"

I'd expected Alex to be the expert on that one. Instead I tried to think of a calm time, a quiet time. Something to help me focus.

I knelt down at Cait's level. She was still on her hands and knees on the path. Ahead of us, through the trees, the creature's mouth was steaming, spluttering Cait's deepest thoughts and secrets into the night.

"Cait," I whispered. "Can you hear me? You've got to empty your mind." I placed one hand on her shoulder and focused.

At once memories fluttered in and out like wings and I zoned in on one humid afternoon. I was kneeling on smooth tatami mats, feeling the sweat gather behind my folded knees. It was a tea ceremony, a summer afternoon.

"Stay close," I murmured to Cait. Then I closed my eyes, hoping she could feel my calm and find her own.

I stripped back my thoughts and focused on the tingling in my legs as blood pumped to my feet. Soft breeze on my skin. The swish of the tea whisk. The hum of water as it boiled inside the smooth grey pot.

I fixed on that afternoon, that one moment. I might have felt Cait's shoulder move, but I wasn't sure, and soon even that disappeared.

The sweetness of cake. The rustle of fabric. Bitter foam on my lips and the smooth, round cup in my hands. I felt my lungs fill, and my nostrils tingled with the sweet tatami smell. I breathed out till my chest was empty and then breathed in again. Everything felt peaceful. Whole. Calm.

I could have stayed that way all night. Perhaps I did.

Then something wound its way into my thoughts. "Miku." Shaking on my shoulder. "Miku!"

It was Alex. "It's gone," he said. "It yelped and took off like it was on fire. It's totally disappeared."

And next to him was Cait. She was standing and smiling.

Cait was back.

CHAPTER EIGHT

I beamed at my curly-headed friend. She was leaning over me and she'd wiped the drool from her face. Life was zinging through her eyes.

"Are you OK, Miku?" she asked. "Did you fall?"

I looked around. The forest was silent but for the hooting of an owl and the rustle of the wind. The black creature, whatever it was, had disappeared. But it wasn't gone without a trace. The air still stank, that same musky smell I'd been smelling for weeks.

I tried to stand but staggered, my legs numb from kneeling. I tried again and this time I made it. "Are you OK?"

"I'm fine," Cait answered. "You're the one who was on the ground."

"She can't remember," Alex said to me, looking sheepish.

"Nothing?" I asked.

"He says there was some sort of monkey," Cait scoffed. "Of course that's a total joke, cos we're..." She paused, looking around. "Where are we, anyway?"

"She remembers nothing," Alex repeated.

"Not even...?" I let my question hang in the air. Did Cait know that the monkey had confessed her crush on Alex?

"Especially not that. And she doesn't need to know." He busied himself with his jacket.

"Know what?" Cait asked.

"You don't remember the black monkey?" I asked.

"What monkey?" Cait grinned. "Come on, Miku. We're not falling for one of Alex's dumb tricks."

"What about the Filth Licker?"

"The what?"

"And the keukegen?"

"The cue-keh-pardon?"

"Demons," Alex helped out. "Our bonfire down at camp created a super-demon. Remember?"

"A super-demon? Try harder, Alex." Cait pushed him on the shoulder. "We're not stupid."

"Cait," I said softly. "You're not going to like this." But it was obvious now. Her memory loss.

That putrid smell, always hanging around. And the way the demons and sprites had been so quick to find us, as if they'd known in advance we'd be coming.

Cait looked up. There was confusion in her eyes, and no wonder. That stinky demon had been sucking at her memories and thoughts, finding out all about us. And there was no gentle way to break the news.

"A demon has been stealing your memories, Cait, controlling your behaviour. And it's probably been happening for a while."

"My what?" Cait spluttered. "Come on, not more demon stories."

"Now do you believe me?" Alex chimed, flopping his floppy fringe in Cait's direction. "I told you there was a monkey demon."

"Why are you ganging up on me?" Cait complained. "Why are you taking his side, Miku?"

"Because it's true," I said gently. "Demons have been reading your mind. I'm sorry. I don't know how much of your memory is missing, or how we'll get it back."

"I don't believe you." Cait looked around, as if she'd just woken up and was on another planet. "What are we doing out here anyway?"

I looked around. I had to agree. Trees towered

over us and the mist was still thick. The woods seemed darker and colder than ever.

"We were out here when it happened," I said. "I'm guessing this creature would usually come to you at night, while you're sleeping, so you'd never usually notice."

"But you've noticed now, right?" Alex said. "Otherwise how'd you get to be in the middle of the woods?" He was looking at Cait kind of funny, as if he was hoping she'd remember for different reasons.

Cait touched the trunk of a tree with one hand. "Perhaps this is all a dream, perhaps I'm still asleep in my bed."

"This isn't a dream." Alex flopped his fringe again, and stared at Cait with big, dopey eyes. "We're on a mission, and we need you."

"What? You're acting like a mutant," Cait said. "So maybe you're right. Maybe this isn't a dream..."

I held my breath. Was she remembering?

"...because it feels more like a nightmare," Cait said. She made a face at Alex and turned to grin at me, but I couldn't grin back.

Alex leapt forward and grabbed a handful of Cait's hair in one hand. He yanked hard.

"Owww! What you do that for?" Cait spun and swung at Alex with both arms. He dropped her hair and tried to spring free, but not before I heard Cait's hand connect with his head. Thud.

"Ow!"

I held my breath. Would there be a spirit echo? But the trees were silent. Alex spun away from Cait, scrambling behind me to where he was safe. He was protecting one eye with his hand.

"Chicken," Cait taunted, circling him. "You started it. Come and fight."

"No way." Alex was still holding his face.

Cait rubbed her scalp where Alex had pulled her hair. "Pulling hair is dumb, even for you."

"So is punching me." Alex circled, staying safely behind me.

"But you pulled my hair."

"Did it hurt?"

"'Course it hurt."

"Then it can't be a dream," Alex announced, grinning despite his sore eye. "This must be reality."

"I'll teach you reality." Cait lunged. I dodged and spun round in time to see Alex and Cait both crashing to the ground, fists flying. Great. So now they were fighting each other. And we still had a super-demon to deal with. Perfect.

I could watch my friends pummel themselves out of being useful. Or try to stop them somehow.

I chose option two. And I used the best weapon I had.

"Cait," I said. "We know you like Alex."

Cait stopped fighting and looked up, her face a careful blank. Alex took the chance to wriggle from her grip.

"What?" she said, looking indignant.

"We know you like him." I nodded in Alex's direction. "We know you count the seats to where he sits."

"I can't stand him," Cait snapped. "You know that. Look!" She threatened to punch Alex again. He rolled out of her reach and scrambled to his feet.

"We know everything, Cait," I said. "We heard it all, from the monkey."

Cait narrowed her eyes.

"Do we have to do this?" Alex was plaintive behind me.

I ignored him. "We know you don't like lasagne, we know you're getting a blister, and we know you've liked Alex for ages, how you adore his fringe, how you think he's so handsome and clever…"

"All right," Alex mumbled. "She gets it."

Cait's face flushed with outrage, then embarrassment, then shock. "A monkey told you this?" She stared into the forest, avoiding Alex's floppy-fringed gaze.

"This demon has been stealing your memories," I said, "and changing your behaviour."

"And since you obviously don't remember," Alex said, "we're here on a mission. We're walking to a farm. To hunt a super-demon."

"Was that it?" Cait asked, dazed.

"What?"

"The monkey whatsit. Was that the super-thing we were hunting?"

I shook my head. "Whatever we're hunting has just been created, and it's already more powerful than the monkey demon. And it's growing stronger. We need to find it and fight it, tonight. Which means we need you to keep going." I felt awful. Poor Cait had lost so many of her memories, and now I was asking her to walk into danger again.

"But that monkey demon, won't it be back?" Cait searched the misty shadows, as if every tree was hiding danger.

"If it does come back, you'll be safe," I said. "It's lost its hold on you. When you emptied your mind, it had nothing left to feed on. It can't use you any more."

"But this is crazy." Cait looked confused. "This kind of stuff doesn't happen."

"It's already happened. Don't you remember the snow? Mrs Okuda? Her flying head?" I stared at my friend, hoping she'd understand.

"Not really…" Cait sneaked a peek at Alex. He was a few steps away, dabbing gingerly at his eye.

"Don't worry," I whispered. "He hardly heard a thing. And you can always pretend you were just making it up."

"OK, yeah." Cait nodded, looking more cheerful. "So, assuming all this is true, when do I get my memories back?"

I looked at the leafy floor. "I don't know. You'll just have to trust us."

CHAPTER NINE

I felt as if the forest was watching us, and waiting. We needed to get moving, but I had to double-check something first.

We'd managed to banish the monkey demon, and Cait was freed from his telepathic powers, though her memory still hadn't returned. But still I wanted to be certain. Was Cait really Cait? Maybe the monkey demon wasn't the only reason for her odd behaviour.

"You could be a Shape Shifter," I explained.

"What?"

"Well, there's still a chance that you're in disguise, that you've taken the real Cait and you're actually a demon fox or badger or something."

"That's rubbish," Cait snorted. "Anyone can see I'm not a demon."

"That's the thing," I explained. "Remember the demon who looked like your dad?"

Cait stamped her feet. "No. Remember I don't remember? Anyway, if I was a demon, wouldn't I have attacked you by now?"

"You already did," Alex said, still tending to his eye. "I bet you're just waiting for the right moment to finish us off. Or maybe you're leading us into a trap."

"Great, so now *you* think I'm a demon too," Cait said. "How do we find out? How can I prove I'm me?"

"You know, this eye is going black, O'Neill," Alex interrupted. "I can feel it. How am I s'posed to notice your new haircut with one eye swollen shut?"

"Alex," I snapped. "Please."

"You noticed my haircut?" Cait said, running a hand through her curls and rubbing at the bit Alex had yanked. "Thanks for not ripping out too much."

"No problem," Alex said, giving a little bow.

I cringed. That monkey demon had a lot to answer for.

"Sorry about your eye," Cait said. "Can I take a look?"

They walked into a beam of starlight and Cait peered at Alex's eye. I tried to ignore them and think.

I knew Cait wasn't a noppera-bō, because I'd seen her reflection in the shower block mirror. But how could I make sure she wasn't a shape-changing fox or badger in disguise?

A wave of light snapped through the sky, hurting my eyes. I cried out, diving to the ground to avoid whatever threat had arrived.

"Oh yeah, it's pretty swollen," Cait said. "We should put that on ice."

I blinked and looked up, bright lights still floating before my eyes. I expected to see some terrible demon looming overhead. Instead there were dark treetops, plus patterned starlight and a tiny slice of moon. And of course, bright torchlight, coming from Cait. She was holding Alex's torch. And it was switched on.

"What are you doing?" I scrambled up, brushing mud and dirt from my jeans. "Did you point that in my face?"

"Only by mistake. Look, Miku, Alex's eye is really swollen. Do you think he'll be OK?"

I couldn't believe it. "Turn it off. You've ruined our night vision. Now everything knows exactly where we are." Sprites and Shape Shifters weren't the only things that could be hiding in the trees. There could be real badgers, or angry boars, or flying cockroaches.

No point in lighting ourselves up like free dinners.

"But first, what do you think?" Cait waved the torch in Alex's direction, sending leery shadows dancing through the trees.

I had to remind myself that Cait couldn't remember any of the dangers we were facing, so it wasn't her fault she was acting so foolish. I needed to concentrate on other things, but to keep Cait quiet I took a quick look at Alex's eye. The surrounding skin was swollen and blue, but the eye itself looked fine. "He'll be OK," I said, turning away. The torchlight sent shattered strips of Alex's shadow through the fog. My brain started working. Shadows.

"What about you?" I asked Cait. "Are you OK, after the fight? Don't you think we should check?"

"What do you mean? He hardly touched me," Cait boasted.

"Just in case," I said, ignoring her protests and leading her into a relatively flat bit where the trees weren't so thick. Then I grabbed Alex's torch, and pointed it so her body threw a long shadow across the leaf-littered ground. "Alex," I demanded. "What kind of shadow is she making?"

"What?" Alex and Cait echoed like forest demons.

"Can you check? What shape is her shadow? And Cait, stay still. Don't turn round."

Alex looked at me as if I was loopy, but peered at Cait's shadow all the same. Cait tapped her foot. "This better be good, Miku."

My heart thumped as we waited.

"It's an ordinary shadow," Alex said. "Shaped like Cait, only taller and slimmer and much better looking."

"Argh." Cait threatened to punch Alex, and he grinned like a goofball.

"Does she have tails?" I prompted. "Is her nose pointy? Are her ears perked?"

"Miku," Cait complained. "Do you have to?"

"No, no and no," said Alex. "Just an ordinary shadow. Completely human. No tail, no pointy nose, no nothing..."

I grinned so hard starlight must have shone from my teeth. Cait was Cait. Her memory had gone, but at least she was herself, not a Shape Shifter or a demon in disguise. We were going to be OK.

"...Not like Mr James's," Alex continued. "Now his was crazy."

My relief choked. "Mr James's shadow?"

"He cast this really creepy shadow, down at the bonfire," Alex said. "I was watching. It was less like a person, and more like a…."

"Fox," guessed Cait. "So that's why you were checking my shadow for tails."

I nodded. Even when they're shape-changed, spirits can't control all the laws of physics. When someone is possessed by a fox demon, their body might look human, but their shadow is still shaped like a fox.

"What about Mr James?" Alex asked. "Was he…?"

I nodded as pieces fell into place. Mr James had said there were no other bookings at camp, which meant our class had been there all alone. And it was Mr James who had collected all the wood for the bonfire, and Mr James who had arranged for the Hyaku Monogatari. Plus his cooking was horrendous, worse than anything we'd expected. "Mr James wasn't Mr James," I guessed. "The demons must've known we were coming."

Alex groaned and Cait fiddled with her torch before looking up. "It was probably me. That monkey, you said it could read my thoughts. Anything I used to know, our plans, our weaknesses… These demons probably know it too."

We were silent after that. Even the wind seemed to stop in the trees. An owl passed overhead, blocking the moon and plunging our clearing into a moment of darkness.

"If they read Cait's mind," Alex said, "then they knew we were coming to camp…"

"And so they took the real Mr James and planted a Shape Shifter in his place, to lead us astray." I was thinking out loud. "They knew we'd try to hunt whatever the Hyaku Monogatari created. They knew we'd sneak away."

"So whatever's at the farm, it's expecting us," Cait ventured.

"Just like the tofu guy," Alex said. "They've all been expecting us, from the beginning."

Alex was right, they were both right. And that meant we were walking into serious trouble. Probably a trap.

"But why us?" Cait asked. "Why do these demons follow you, Miku?"

I looked down at my hands. Why did they follow me? Was it something I'd done? Something I'd forgotten to do? Was it my family, the supposedly powerful Takeshita clan? But we'd never had these troubles before. Not while Baba was alive and Zashiko lived in our house. "I don't know," I answered. "I'm just hoping that we can get them to stop."

"So what do we do?"

"We keep going," I said.

What else could we do? Even if the demons were expecting us, even if the whole thing was a set-up....

If we walked away now, the Hyaku Monogatari and the evil it had created would only grow stronger. Plus it was too late to turn back. We were halfway there already, all alone in the middle of the woods.

"We have to face them," I went on. "Fight them." I looked beyond our ring of torchlight to where the forest loomed, swallowing all brightness into its gloomy branches. "We've got to give it our best shot." I paused, checking for Cait's reaction, and she nodded. Beside her, Alex was nodding too.

"Let's switch off that torch and get our night vision back," I said. "We're going to need it."

Cait nodded again and I heard the torch click. We were thrust at once into darkness.

CHAPTER TEN

We'd been walking for hours, probably half the night, and the forest was changing around us once more. Now everything was slick with black moss and heavy with dew. Tree trunks were slathered with moulds and lichens, giant mushrooms seemed to leap from the ground. I guessed the sun hadn't shone here for years.

I didn't know how far we had come, or how far we still had to go, and the dread of walking into the unknown was taking its toll. I was tired and hungry and scared. Above us the silver moon hung like a blade and the forest was so cold I could feel a chill creeping closer to my heart.

"Gross," Alex muttered. "This is disgusting."

He had skipped ahead and was wiping moss off his hands on to his shirt. The blackness seemed to slide across his skin like oil on water. I could see dark stains growing across his shirt and skin, spreading like ink.

"Better leave it," I said. "We don't know what it is. There could be poison ivy all along here." Alex flopped his fringe at me and then I noticed his open collar. "Your pearl, it's gone."

Alex's hand went to his throat. "What? Oh, yeah. It must've fallen off back in the forest."

"A pearl? Aren't you worried?" Cait asked. "We could go back to look for it…"

"No, we could not," I interrupted. "We don't have time." We had to find the super-demon, defeat it and get back to camp in time for breakfast. The schedule was too tight to go jewellery shopping.

Cait looked at the floor. "Sorry about that," she said. "It must've fallen off when we were fighting."

"Don't worry about it," Alex said, and he danced ahead, down the path.

It had to be three or four in the morning, and we'd been walking all night, but Alex didn't seem a bit tired. He was probably fuelled by love, I thought, grimacing. He and Cait were getting on better now that Cait had confessed that she liked him and punched him in the eye. I wondered what might happen between them if we got through tonight alive.

Or if Cait ever got her memories back.

Something shrieked, jagged and eerie, from somewhere not so far away, making me jump. Then another shriek rang through the forest, a siren call, as if something was hunting.

"Is that it?" Cait asked, her eyes wide.

"Maybe," I said, hoping I was wrong.

"Maybe it's just a forest animal," Alex suggested. "An owl or something?"

But the shrieking had sealed it for me. Those were happy hunting shrieks. Killing shrieks. In that instant I had realised we weren't hunting a super-demon. We were hunting super-demons. There was more than one. And they weren't forest animals, or at least, they weren't any more.

"What do we do, Miku?" Cait breathed.

"Track them," I said, gulping. "We must be nearly there."

The calls didn't go away, they kept echoing through the trees, leading us through the mossy thickets to a place where the forest seemed to grow thinner, dryer. I ignored the twisting in my gut, a feeling that screamed out to turn around, run away. I just put one foot in front of the other, walking in silence, waiting for the next shriek to slice through the night.

Alex was leading the way, but even he had run out of things to say.

"Firewood," he grunted at last, pointing at a stack of wood that stood ready and waiting for the winter. Tree stumps poked through the ground all around us, as silent as gravestones in the sand.

"We must be close," Cait said hopefully.

"But which way now?" Alex asked. Ahead of us the forest floor was criss-crossed with options. He skipped on, scouting like a dog, but I wasn't so sure. I hung back with Cait, listening for the next eerie call.

But the next sound didn't come from the supernatural super-demons; it came from Alex.

"I can see it," he cried. "The farm."

Were we really there? Cait and I ran the last few metres, following Alex down the winding path and across the forest border into a stretch of cleared land.

A field. A farm. Yes. We'd really made it.

But my excitement didn't last. Where were the cows? Where were the tractors? I'd at least been expecting a WELCOME mat at the front door. Or a farmer, and maybe a whole army of farmer's children. I'd been hoping for help. But the place was deserted and probably had been for years. There wasn't a single car or cow or farmer to be seen. Just some weedy fields, two broken barns, and one derelict farmhouse.

We were on our own. And worse, the shrieking had stopped. Either the shriekers had moved on or they knew we were there, and they were watching.

"Stick together," I whispered. "Stay close. We have to search."

"What're we searching for?" Cait asked.

"We'll know when we find them."

"Them?"

"There's more than one," I admitted. "Probably three."

"Three?" Cait echoed. "Three super-demons?"

I nodded.

"No problem," Alex grinned, his voice falsely bright. "If there's three of us, and three of them, then it'll be just like basketball. Plus we've got you, Miku, with your powers and stuff. We should be fine."

I wanted to snap at him, to remind him that this wasn't a game. But we needed all the optimism we could get, and it was too late in the night to start arguing again. We had to be a team.

"Let's stick together," I said, remembering the last time Cait and I had split up. I'd had fireballs thrown at me, been attacked by living curtains, and nearly been eaten by my supply teacher. I didn't want to repeat any of that in a hurry. "Let's search them one at a time," I said, pointing at the dark husk of the closest barn. "That one first."

The first barn was locked, but that didn't matter. We just poked our heads through its rotten walls, shining our torches up and down and scanning for signs of supernatural life. The place was one giant spider's web and the air was rich with dust and ancient dung. My torchlight hit on something small and furry that flashed into the shadows with a squeak, causing dust to rise up like a storm.

Alex jumped, hitting his head on the decaying wall. "What was that?"

"A mouse," I said. "And it's still alive. A good sign."

We gave the first barn the all-clear and headed across a field to the second, keeping our torches switched on and down low. Our lights skipped along the ground, shining on mildewed timber, tussocked grass, piles of dung so old they'd turned to stone. It must have been ages since any farmer had lived here.

"What about the neighbours?" Alex complained, traipsing after me with his torchlight skimming the ground. "Remember? Mr James said someone from the farm had rung about the animal activity, but there's no one here. I bet no one's lived here for years."

"But you told us Mr James wasn't Mr James," said Cait. "That he was some fox demon in disguise. So maybe there was no phone call. Maybe it's just us, and the thing, the shrieking thing."

The shrieking thing that wasn't shrieking any more. I looked around, waiting for something to jump from the bushes and launch at our throats. But nothing moved.

We stood outside the doors to the second barn. These doors were open, gaping like the jaws of a hungry monster.

"Inside?" Cait quivered, standing just beyond the shadow of the barn.

I nodded, and we stepped through the doors, into the darkness.

The gloom melted away beneath our torches. The yellow light streamed through the thick air, shining off dust and dirt, motor oil and metal, empty rafters and silent walls. The floor was thick with spongy mud and rotten hay. And nothing moved, not a bird, not a bat, not even a spider.

"Where are the webs?" Cait's question shivered along the walls. "Where are the mice?"

She was right. You'd think something would be living inside this barn. I swung my torch around, searching for fresh droppings, webs, nests, even a millipede. Any sign that something once lived here. There was nothing. It was as if every living thing had been moved on, or scared off.

Then something stirred from behind us, at the doors of the barn. I swung round in a panic. Whatever it was, it had us trapped. That front door was the only way out.

"*Da-me-da, da-me-da.*" The something spoke. "No good. No good." It was crouched in the open door of the barn, a silhouette in the starlight. It had a small, smooth body, topped with a wave of shaggy hair, and I could just make out its long, hairy tongue.

Cait took one look and screamed so loud my eardrums were ringing.

"*Fushigi-da-ne,*" the thing said. "How very strange." And then it disappeared.

CHAPTER ELEVEN

It was definitely the Filth Licker, or it had been. I'd been expecting the monkey demon, or the super-demons, something evil. But certainly not the aka-na-me. Back at camp he'd been too scared to leave the shower block, let alone travel through the forest all alone. But whatever he'd been, he wasn't any more. He had completely disappeared.

"Was that...?" Alex asked, shining his torch where the red demon had been.

"Sure was," I said.

"Sure was what?" asked Cait.

"You don't remember?" Alex asked.

"No," Cait said, getting frustrated. "But I'm guessing it wasn't the super-demon. It sounded more like my granny."

"It's called a Filth Licker," I explained, walking back to the barn door, the spot we'd last seen the little red demon before he disappeared. "He cleans bathrooms, that sort of thing."

I could feel Cait's eyes grow wider.

"He's quite cool," Alex said, flopping his fringe as if that explained everything.

"And he's gone." I shone my torch around the barn's big doors. There was nothing.

Then, just as suddenly, the Filth Licker reappeared, seeming to materialise from the barn door itself. Cait stepped back, pulling Alex with her.

The red demon blinked at each of us, then turned his attention to his arm, licking until it glistened in our torchlight.

"Where...?" I was too astonished to finish my sentence.

The Filth Licker stopped licking and pushed his lips into a toothy smile. With one shining arm, he pointed at a spot high up on the door. "There."

I looked where he was pointing but could see nothing. Just an ordinary bit of door. "What?"

The red demon shrugged, and then he sprang, using his single-toed legs to launch himself at the door.

I cringed, waiting to hear the sickening crunch

of demon slamming into wood. Instead there was a barely discernible squelch. When I looked, the aka-na-me was stuck halfway up the wall, like a cockroach in a flypaper house. And he was grinning.

"I am uneaten," he crowed. "Not one fox, not one badger. I am safe. I am awesome." He licked one eye and bobbed up and down on his four limbs, never budging from where he hung on the door.

"What are you doing here?" Alex asked. "I thought you didn't want to come?"

The Filth Licker's body waved up and down, rippling like fine silk. "Didn't want to come," he agreed. "But did. Very awesome. Very brave." He did a full body jiggle and then bounced to the floor. Then he took a moment to slick his hair back into place. "You need me," he said. "You need this." From nowhere he whipped a tiny, ceramic jar, stopped with a cork. He held it up as if it was a golden trophy.

"What is it?" I asked.

He looked around, then leaned forward. "From my uncle," he whispered. "It's for you, who set me free." He did a little jig, hopping on the floor as if he was skipping, then suddenly stopped.

"Did you find them?" he whispered.

"Find who?"

"*Da-me-da*. No good. We must search faster," he said.

"Search for what?" I asked. "What are you doing here?"

The demon shuddered, then energetically licked its other arm.

"Let him speak," said Cait. "You're scaring him."

The creature looked up. "Not scared," he said. "Didn't want to come, but did. Very awesome."

"So why are you here?" Cait asked, trying to be gentle.

"Pretty lady," he said. "You need this." And he held up the ceramic jar once again.

"What's it for?" Alex asked.

The Filth Licker's tongue zipped out, combing soft hairs over his eyeballs. "For the kama itachi."

Fear shot through me. He'd actually said it. "The what?"

The red demon leaned forward. "The kama itachi. You will need strong magic to destroy them." He shuddered and launched himself at the barn door, sticking like glue. Then he licked the wood as if there was no tomorrow.

As far as I was concerned, he was probably right. Just then, tomorrow seemed a long and impossible time away.

"What did he say, Miku?" asked Cait.

The kama itachi. I'd guessed as much but to hear it said out loud was a shock. Had the Hyaku Monogatari really created such a horror? Baba had whispered to me about kama itachi. They weren't the kind of thing you discussed in polite company.

"What is it, Miku?" Alex asked. "What's going on?"

I blinked, staring at the Filth Licker. He was still stuck to the door, licking the old wood into a rich shine. I remembered him shivering in the shower block. He had been scared, and rightly so. So why would he face the forest and the kama itachi, why risk his life to bring us a ceramic pot?

"Karma touchy?" Alex laughed. "Like please-do-not-touchy?"

"Alex," I snapped. "This is serious. The kama itachi are Sickle Weasels." I shivered as I said the words.

"Weasels?" Alex scoffed.

Cait frowned. "Weasels aren't so bad."

"We can easily beat a few weasels," Alex grinned. "It's not like they can eat us."

I shook my head. "You don't understand. They're not ordinary weasels. They're Sickle Weasels." I swallowed. "And it's quite likely they'll

123

be wanting to eat us."

Cait and Alex stared. The Filth Licker blinked slowly, then turned his tongue back to licking the door.

"I'm sorry?" Cait said, looking confused.

"They're more like weapons than demons," I said. "Their claws can extend into giant blades, they move faster than the speed of sound…"

"These are weasels we're talking about?" Alex looked disbelieving, but he took a quick glance all around, just the same.

"Like I said, they're not ordinary weasels. They're fast, they're intelligent. And they work together, focusing their powers to control the wind or possess a body, living or dead. Plus they're carnivores. Blood-eaters."

"Do their heads come off?" Alex asked, tilting his own head as if he was weighing up our chances.

"Not this time. They don't need to. Their whole body can whirl through the air faster than you can see, and they'll slash at your arms and legs with their scythes, mining for blood."

"That is so gross," Cait whispered, looking sick.

"And they breed," I continued, "faster than rabbits. If we have three Sickle Weasels, soon we could have hundreds more, all whirling and slashing with their blades. A swarm of Sickle Weasels will attack anything in their path - their enemies, their friends. They're seriously unpleasant."

Cait swallowed. "So I guess we're going to stand in their path, right?"

"Are we sure we want to do that?" Alex zipped his jacket up and down and the sound hummed through the night. "I mean..."

"*Shō ga nai*," said the Filth Licker, still hanging from the now-shining door. "There is no other way." He was looking straight at me. "You must destroy them. Or a plague of kama itachi will be born. And they will kill and kill, growing ever stronger."

Guilt pummelled at my brain. "Did we do this?" I asked him, not wanting the answer. "With the Hyaku Monogatari? Did we create these things?"

But the little demon ignored me, and I didn't really want to hear his answer anyway.

"What do they look like?" Cait asked, searching the sky.

"They look like weasels," said the Filth Licker solemnly.

"Gee, thanks," said Alex.

"You're welcome." The demon puffed out his chest and gave a little dip of his head.

"And how do we destroy them?" Alex asked, looking at me this time.

But what could I say? Kids like us couldn't destroy Sickle Weasels. The kama itachi weren't ordinary demons, the kind with a secret, supernatural weakness. They were super-fast, and extra-dangerous. To destroy a team of Sickle Weasels we'd need a powerful sorcerer, or some sort of secret weapon, one even Baba had never heard of. And we were on a deserted farm on the edge of a wood with zero chance of discovering either.

Then the Filth Licker jumped down from the door. "With this," he said, holding out the ceramic jar with his webbed hand.

I stared. "And this is what exactly?"

The red demon cantered on the spot, thumping his one-toed foot three times. "It's from my uncle," he said. "Very sacred, very special."

"Your uncle?"

The Filth Licker looked bashful, running his hairy tongue over one eye before replying. "The Abura Sumashi," he whispered. "But you mustn't tell."

"Tell what?" Cait asked.

"We've been saving it," whispered the Filth Licker. "He found it in a temple, on the Amakusa Island."

"Found it?" I couldn't help myself. "Stole it more likely." I raised my eyes at Alex and Cait. The Abura Sumashi was a notorious oil thief. A potato-headed straw-covered oil thief. He looked more like a bumblebee than a powerful sorcerer. But perhaps sacred oil could help us… "So what good is this oil in fighting Sickle Weasels?"

"Fire," said the Filth Licker, bobbing up and down. "When their nest is burned, the weasels will be furious. Their spirits will melt into nothing. Lamp oil makes good fire."

Sacred fire from sacred oil. It might just work. Except for one problem. We didn't have the nest.

Then Cait called us into the back of the barn. "Over here," she said. "I think I've found something."

CHAPTER TWELVE

Right at the back of the barn, hidden by old farm equipment and shadows, Cait had spotted it. A cleared patch on the floor, swept into the shape of a circle. Where the rest of the barn floor was thick with mud and dust and rotten hay, this circle was lined with fur: the skins of small animals, some so tiny they could have come from key-ring teddy bears. In the centre of the circle was a clutch of eggs, maybe two dozen in all, arranged in three interlinking rings.

"*Kore desu,*" the Filth Licker confirmed, nodding. "This is it."

"The Weasels' nest," Alex breathed.

"Eggs?" Cait said. "Weasels don't have eggs."

"Weasels don't have blades coming out of their legs either," I reminded her.

128

"S'pose not," she said, still staring at the glowing, pulsing eggs.

I felt ill just looking at them. The eggs seemed to beat in time, as if they were pumping poison into the air. And the nest that cradled them was lined with dozens of animal skins. No wonder there was nothing left living in this barn.

"So now what?" Cait asked.

"We take the oil," I said, gesturing at the ceramic jar the Filth Licker was holding. "And we burn it. All the eggs. The whole nest. Everything."

Everyone nodded but nobody moved. I guess we were all thinking the same thing. "We can't burn it in here," Cait said, looking around. "The whole barn could go up."

"We need to move the nest," Alex agreed. "Burn it outside."

"What about the kama itachi?" I argued. "They'll be somewhere about. If we're outside they'll spot us as soon as we light the first match."

"They'll spot us just as fast if the barn burns down," Alex reasoned, and I had to agree.

"How will you move it?" the Filth Licker asked, still clinging to his jar of sacred oil.

Then I realised everyone was looking at me. "How will *I* move it?"

But there was no point in arguing. Someone had to touch the disgusting nest, and the little demon was right. It might as well be me. I pulled down the sleeves of my jacket, not wanting any part of me to touch the nest more than was necessary. Even so, it looked as if I would have to make several trips.

Then I had an idea, and I took my jacket off completely, laying it flat on the ground. "I'll slide my jacket under it," I said. "Then I'll just drag the whole thing along the ground."

Using my jacket as a sledge meant I wouldn't have to transport the nest bit by disgusting bit. Of course I would still have to touch it, but only enough to slip my jacket underneath. I wiped my hands on my jeans, as if they were already soiled.

"I'll help," Alex said unexpectedly. "I'll slide your jacket under. You lift the nest."

I nodded. Alex wasn't so bad now we knew him better. I felt warmer, despite being jacketless. "Thanks, Alex. On the count of three."

I didn't want to touch it, not any of it. I was scared it might be electric or poisonous or worse. But on three I slipped my fingers under, and lifted one rich furry edge, just enough for Alex to slide my jacket in. The nest felt velvety and almost warm, as if the animal skins were still alive. I lowered the edge back down and checked: the eggs were still in place, still pulsing. They hadn't budged. It was as if they were held in place, cemented to their rings of power.

"Ready?" Alex asked.

"Ready," I nodded, and we each grabbed an edge of my jacket and pulled. The entire nest moved, sliding along as if my jacket were some kind of magic carpet.

"Keep going," Alex said. So we dragged the nest and its evil eggs across the floor and out of the barn. We slid it all the way across the grass, to a spot where the flames wouldn't reach the buildings. Cait and the Filth Licker trailed close behind.

"Are you sure?" Cait asked, looking around. "There's nothing out here, not even a tree to hide behind. If they come we'll have nowhere to hide."

"Then we'll have to be quick," Alex said. He was getting excited, I could see. "Who's got the oil?"

"Here," said the Filth Licker, holding up the unmarked jar. The sacred oil.

"Won't we need wood or something?" Cait asked.

I shook my head, hugging myself against the cold. "Once it's alight, the oil will burn," I said. "It won't need extra fuel."

131

"What about your jacket?" Cait asked. It was still under the Sickle Weasels' nest.

I shrugged. Already the tips of my fingers and ears were freezing, but I didn't want to wear that jacket ever again. "I'll get another."

"Quick," Alex said. "Let's get the fire started."

I nodded, but something was bugging me. Something wasn't right. Yet Alex was correct. We didn't have time to mess about. If we lit the fire now, we could be away before the Weasels even knew we had arrived. Every second we delayed was an extra moment we could be discovered.

"OK," I breathed. "Let's do it. Who has the oil?"

The Filth Licker reached across, the ceramic jar in his red hand. The jar was heavier than I'd imagined and seemed to have an energy of its own. It was almost warm against the cold night. I wished we could keep it. It could help keep me warm on the return journey.

Instead I wrenched at the cork and it popped, filling the air with the rich smell of lamp oil. Then I stood over the nest, struck with a sudden confusion. How did this work exactly? A ritual to melt evil spirits into nothing? I'd never heard of such a thing, not even from Baba. Did we need to say some sort of prayer?

"Hurry, Miku," Alex hissed. "They could be coming."

Something still didn't seem right. "Don't you think…?"

"Miku," Alex was urgent. "We don't have time. Look at the others, they're scared. You have to act now."

I glanced across at Cait and the Filth Licker. They did look scared. And it was my fault they were out here, my fault that they were in danger. So in the end I didn't think, and I didn't wait.

I took a deep breath and poured the entire contents of the jar over the skins and the eggs and the nest. The oil spilled like golden rain across the beating eggs, pooling in circular droplets on the hairs and furs. It was done. Now all we needed was a light.

"Matches," I said.

The Filth Licker blinked.

"Please," I prompted, glancing at the sky. What if the Weasels saw we were here?

"Not me," the demon said, looking bashful. "I can't make fire."

"You brought oil but no matches?" I couldn't believe it. What about the others? "Cait? Alex?"

Alex looked down, fumbling with his jacket.

Cait shook her head. "Sorry."

"You've got to be kidding. No one even has a lighter? Nothing?" I scanned the sky again. The Sickle Weasels were out there somewhere, and they wouldn't be happy to find their future generations doused in oil. We had to light this fire, and fast. Perhaps we could rub two sticks together?

I flashed my torch across the ground. It was time for Plan B. "Maybe we do need wood," I said. "Perhaps we could…"

Then I heard the sound of flames. Roaring flames. I looked down at the Sickle Weasels' nest and had to jump back. The fire was lit. The furs were burning and the glowing, pulsing eggs were already cracking and cooking, on their way to scrambled destruction. But how? And who?

I looked around for Cait, but she'd retreated behind me, and the Filth Licker was with her, trembling on his single toes. They were staring at Alex, mouths open, saying nothing.

And Alex was standing there, just beyond the fire. There was a wily grin on his face and his blackened eye was shining through the flames. "The fire is burning," he said. "My work here is done."

The bottom fell from my stomach. We were in serious trouble. Because although it was Alex's body standing beside the fire, and Alex's face smiling across at me, I was pretty sure that Alex didn't have a brown bushy tail. Or make that tails.

I could count at least three enormous tails poking out from under Alex's jacket. In the growing light of the oil fire, I could also see the strange shape his shadow was casting. The flames flickered as they roared, but our mistake was clear: the long nose, the pointy ears.

"You?" I gasped. "You're a Shape Shifter?"

Alex grinned. Then his body shuddered and melted before my eyes, falling into a tiny fur-ball with tufts of black hair, still dressed in Alex's jacket. And there, grinning at me with its beady demon eyes, was the fur-ball we'd seen way back at the shower block. The keukegen. The demon that Alex had spotted. But who had spotted who?

Before I could blink, the keukegen's tiny body was changing again. Hair fell away and his body grew taller, stretching like the flames that burned beside us. His belly blossomed into a giant gut that stretched Alex's jacket to bursting. "Welcome, Takeshita-san," said a familiar voice. "Welcome to our little trap."

Mr James? But it wasn't. Not the real Mr James. Because this Mr James began to melt again. More hair grew, his arms and legs grew shorter, his ears perked. This time when the creature stopped changing he stood before me in his true form, shrugging himself free of Alex's clothes. It was a huge brown fox, with three massive tails and two eyes, twinkling maliciously.

"What are you?" I asked him. "What trap?"

But I didn't get an answer. The Shape Shifter bared its teeth, then slapped at the ground with its tails. Sparks erupted into the night, and something cried out from above, curdling the air. It was half joy, half despair, and it sent shivers across my heart. It was the Sickle Weasels. They were back.

CHAPTER THIRTEEN

Above us the sky erupted. Shrieking, flames, fierce winds and worst nightmares. Fire rippled across the burning nest, waves of heat shimmering into the sky. The flames had seized upon the tiny furs and the eggs they protected. Hairs and shells were melting, yolks and skins were vaporising. The fire consumed the nest with a violence that shut out all else.

Almost.

Above me I could hear them, shrieking and hissing, circling their burning nest over and again. The kama itachi, the Sickle Weasels. They sounded well and truly enraged. They must have spotted us as soon as the first flames hit the sky, and now they were circling so fast I couldn't separate them. Flashes of whirling Weasel came in and out of view as they zipped around, and I caught the steely glint of sickles reflecting the fire's light.

They had us. We were out in the open, with nowhere to run. I cursed the Alex-fox. He'd led us here, to this farm and to this empty paddock, then he'd run off as soon as things heated up. Our only hope was the sacred fire: could it melt the Weasels' spirits before their bodies sliced us into salad?

I cursed myself for not seeing sooner. I should have guessed that Alex was an impostor. He had walked all night without getting tired. He hadn't flinched when he'd lost his precious pearl in the forest. And when I'd checked Cait's shadow in the torchlight, I hadn't thought to check Alex's as well. How long had he been a fox?

And what about Mr James? And the keukegen? The brown fox had been busy. And of course I should have seen it. When the shower block lights went out, the keukegen had disappeared seconds before Mr James had so tidily arrived. A fox can only possess one thing at a time, so for Mr James to show up, the keukegen had to go. Which meant the real Alex must have been with us down at the shower block, since he'd been around at the same time as the fake keukegen and the fake Mr James.

So where was the real Alex? And what about the

real Mr James? Where had the fox taken them?

I gasped as the winds pushed me forward. Dust and sticks leapt into the air, whipping up and around and away, but I didn't feel a single cut from the Sickle Weasels' blades. I blinked through the grit in my eyes. Why weren't they attacking? Something was keeping their sickles at bay.

I searched for the Alex-fox. Maybe he was on our side after all, somehow holding the Sickle Weasels back? He must have heard what the Filth Licker said - that the sacred oil would create a sacred fire, strong enough to melt the kama itachi spirits into nothing. And he'd encouraged us, lit the fire. So maybe he *was* on our side.

I clung on to that hope as the air around us began to whirl. The storm was growing stronger and I was battling to stay upright. The Sickle Weasels were still zooming around, keeping the fire at the centre of their fury. Then I realised: they weren't fighting, they were preparing. They were building a hurricane, maybe hoping to blow out the fire and protect their nest, to save their spirits from melting.

I looked around for Cait and the Filth Licker. They had been blown metres forward and the little demon was almost airborne in the storm. Cait grabbed his webbed hand and staggered in my direction, doubled over against the wind, shielding her face from flying sticks and dust.

The hurricane was growing, but the fire was still burning, its flames tossing high and straight into the night sky, as if there were no winds at all.

Cait called to me but I heard nothing. Her voice was consumed by the roaring of the fire and the wind and the kama itachi's rage. I braced myself and reached across to her with one hand. "Grab on." But I knew she couldn't hear me. Leaves and sand battered my body and the storm fought to drag me up and away.

Suddenly the whole world seemed to be whirling around and upwards. The entire night was orbiting around us. Through the blur of the winds I could see only flashes of the Sickle Weasels, their blades whizzing through the air.

"Meet you halfway," I screamed at Cait, and my words were whipped away by the storm. Branches and stones pelted my body and I saw the same bit of tree whirl past again and again. Something black hurtled towards me. The Filth Licker's jar? I ducked and hoped and it tumbled overhead, clipping my ear as it rode the winds towards the kama itachi's blades.

Someone screamed, piercing the night.

It was Cait. She was crouched low and bracing herself against the hurricane's pull. And she was alone. She cried out again, reaching into the storm with one empty hand.

Seconds later something squealed as it went whirling past. I caught a glimpse of shiny red, of curly black. The Filth Licker. He was tumbling through the winds, being sucked up into the blades of the Sickle Weasels' storm.

Our fire was still burning but the Weasels were showing no sign of melting into destruction. We had to do something fast, rescue the Filth Licker, get to safety. I had no idea how long the fire would take to do its work. I crouched and tensed, focused on staying low and heavy. Wind flicked hair like a whip across my eyes. Rocks and sticks pelted me like sideways rain. And I took a tiny step towards Cait.

But Cait was distracted, reaching for me with one hand and with the other reaching for the aka-na-me as he tumbled by above us. The Alex-fox was nowhere to be seen.

I snatched another look at the fire: the nest was still burning, glowing blue with charcoal and ash. How much longer would it take? Surely soon, very soon, the heat and flames would begin to melt the kama itachi into nothing. But would that be soon enough?

The flames were smaller now. Columns of blue smoke whispered straight into the night sky.

Above us the Sickle Weasels were a glowing blur of slashing steel and whirling fur. Their shrieking never stopped and they stirred and stirred the whirlwind, drawing everything in and around and ever higher.

Then, almost as I watched, the storm changed, focusing in on itself. Where once the winds had raged around the fire, they now seemed to centre on it, weaving a basket of air around and through and under the blue flames and their burning nest.

Gradually, the fire began to rise, along with the nest and the eggs and all that the flames had touched. The whole bundle began spinning slowly, almost majestically, through the air.

The Sickle Weasels were reclaiming their nest. Or what was left of it. This is their last effort, I thought. Their dying breath. We've nearly got them.

I forgot about trying to reach Cait or saving the Filth Licker. Instead I watched the charred nest as it burned in mid air. Bits of smouldering fur fell away, glowing blue and tumbling to the ground. Then an egg dropped, whirling once around the circle before smashing down to earth. All that was left of the nest was glowing charcoal, articulated ash. Surely we had beaten them now.

The nest gave one last and gracious turn through the air, then collapsed into a hundred tiny pieces of blackened fur and burning shell. I watched the sky, waiting for a sign that we'd won.

And almost at once the winds slowed, as if the air had thickened into fermented beans. Sticks and rocks began dropping from the sky. I heard a cry as the Filth Licker landed on the ground, and another as the empty jar was dumped on his head. The little demon was safe.

The sky cleared and when I looked there wasn't a sickle in sight. It was just as the Filth Licker had said. The kama itachi were gone, the sacred fire had melted their spirits into nothing. And perhaps they would never come back. It was over. We had done it. I felt like crying.

Now our only problem was that a fox had been masquerading as Alex and Mr James, so the real Alex and Mr James probably needed rescuing. And of course Oscar was still rotting in the Sick Bay.

I sighed, watching the last of the eggs smoulder on the ground. I'd had enough of demon hunting for one night. Maybe our teachers would take responsibility for finding the real Mr James when the fake one didn't come back, and maybe Oscar would be cured now that the kama itachi were defeated.

And as for Alex? I figured the shape-shifting fox could keep Alex, at least for a couple of days, just until Cait and I had warmed up and had a good sleep and eaten a few good meals. I sighed again, thinking how good the camp food would be once the real Mr James was back in the kitchen.

Then, right beside me, something hissed.

I spun round. And suddenly Alex wasn't the focus of my attention any more. Mostly because he wasn't in front of me, growling and gnashing his teeth and threatening to rip out my throat. Unlike Cait.

I stared at my friend. She thrashed her nails at me, quivering and drooling. Then she shrieked. A Weasel shriek.

And then I realised. The fire hadn't melted the kama itachi into nothing. We'd been tricked, we were horribly wrong. The power of the fire had melted them together. Their spirits had united and now they had found a new home.

Cait had turned strangely green. Her mouth was stretched, as if stuffed with too many marshmallows, and she had hunched her shoulders like the hackles of a wolf.

I looked around for help. The Filth Licker had landed a few metres away, on the other side of what had once been our fire. He was picking leaves from his hair and checking his shiny limbs for broken bones, but he didn't seem hurt. And he wasn't hissing or drooling. Unlike Cait. I checked for Alex. Or the Alex-Mr-James-fox. But there was no sign of either, and now wasn't really a great time for a reunion.

Cait hissed at me and slashed the air with one hand. Slowly, inching forward on careful feet, she began to stalk me.

I tried to match her pace, edging slowly backwards. "Cait? Are you in there?"

CHAPTER FOURTEEN

So things weren't going all that well. The sacred fire had been a massive failure, uniting our enemies instead of melting them. A pyromaniac, shape-changing fox had kidnapped Alex. And now Cait was drooling and hissing and possessed by some very angry Sickle Weasels. That left me and a two-toed Filth Licker who was desperately scared. And he wasn't the only one.

I stepped backwards, away from Cait, trying to think on my feet. With their spirits united, the Sickle Weasels were powerful enough to possess another body. No wonder the Alex-fox had been so keen to light the fire.

My best friend was now crouched in attack

mode, stalking slowly forward with her claws out and teeth bared. I kept stepping backwards, willing myself to think clearly. There had to be a way out of this mess.

Cait screeched at me and stole forward, eyes flashing.

"Hello? Cait?" I backed away, shivering against the cold. The only thing I could think was to reach out to my friend. Perhaps I could try to talk her out, like with the monkey demon and the tea ceremony. Perhaps…

Cait growled from the back of her throat, then chirped three times, tossing her head as if trying to clear something from her ears. When she looked up, her eyes weren't hers any more. They were white, and round as moons. "You cannot save her, Takeshita-san."

I jumped back, trembling. Cait had spoken, but not with Cait's voice. From her mouth had come a guttural sound, like crunching gravel in a graveyard. But whatever had spoken, it knew my surname.

"Who are you?" I demanded. "Leave Cait alone."

The Cait-weasel laughed, a half-hissing, half-barking that I guessed was a very bad sign.

"Let her go?" it crowed. "Why should we? We've been using her for weeks. Our satori has been visiting her in the nights, reading her mind, stealing her memories and reporting them back." Cait snarled and crept forward. "And our fox has worked hard for this moment, masquerading as the camp man, and as the boy you call Alex. We have you now, Takeshita-san. Your friends cannot save you this time."

The Cait-weasel sprang, fingernails out and teeth bared. I lurched backwards, tripping in the grass and landing with a thump on my tailbone. When I hit the ground I rolled sideways, scrambling to my feet with a wary eye on Cait.

So we'd been right about the mind-reading monkey demon. Nice to know, but it didn't make me feel better about being eaten alive by my best friend.

I sneaked a peek behind me, spotting the Filth Licker quivering under a tree. He seemed utterly terrified, but he was alive, and he was all I had left. A filth-licking demon might not be the most glamorous sidekick, but at least he was in possession of his own body. And as Baba used to say, a single arrow is more easily broken. I reversed in his direction, hoping we'd find some strength in numbers. The Cait-weasel paced towards me as I backed away.

"There is nowhere to run, Takeshita-san.

The tofu boy is rotting. The Alex boy is our prisoner. And even the pretty aka-na-me has betrayed you."

My gut did a flip and I glanced at the shivering Filth Licker. His eyes were wide and he shook his head at me vehemently. Were the Weasels telling the truth? Had the Filth Licker betrayed us?

"Surprised, Takeshita-san?" The kama itachi turned Cait's voice into a sneer.

I swung back to look at Cait. Her eyes surged with white and flecks of foam were appearing in the corners of her mouth.

"What did you think that oil was? Told you it was from his uncle, did he?"

I staggered backwards, away from everything she was saying.

"You walked so kindly into our trap, Takeshita child." Cait grinned and licked her lips. "That was not ordinary oil. It was residue, gathered over generations, the remains of long-dead spirits scraped one by one from the leaves and the lives of the forest. A piece of everyone who was ever lost had been concentrated into that jar. So thank you, Takeshita-san. If you hadn't burned our nest with that oil, we could never have united." The Cait-weasel laughed, chirping as if she had swallowed a bird.

Spirit residues? So we'd burned bits of long-gone spirit when we set fire to the kama itachi's nest. We'd been set up. The Filth Licker had betrayed me. Everyone had betrayed me. I had nowhere left to go.

"What about your spirits?" I asked, desperate. "Don't you want to rest?"

"We serve our master now," the Sickle Weasels' gravel voice answered through Cait's mouth. "Our spirits are indebted."

"But your nest is gone," I argued, treading ever backwards. "You have no reason to stay. Your spirits can be free."

"You took our freedom," the voice roared. "You, Takeshita-san, you contributed to our creation. You told your story at the Hyaku Monogatari. You poured the sacred oil. Your powers are now woven into ours. Destroy us and you must also destroy yourself."

"But I didn't…" I tried to protest. I hadn't told a story at the bonfire ritual. I had only told the truth, tried to warn everybody away.

"Your words were part of the ritual and your story is one of the hundred." The kama itachi flashed behind Cait's eyes. "Even you cannot destroy us now."

I stepped backwards and stumbled. Behind me I could see the despicable Filth Licker, still quivering under the tree. The kama itachi were right. Even the little red demon had betrayed me. There was no one else. I was going to be eaten alive on an abandoned farm. I would never see my family again. Mum, Dad, little Kazu. I felt tears prick my eyes. I'd never sit round the dinner table telling Mum and Dad about school. I'd never have to bath Kazu or change his stinky nappy. I'd never again see my little brother's grin or hear his silly laugh. My throat burned and I blinked tears from my eyes. I'd be with Baba soon. And then I remembered. Zashiko.

Zashiko had protected us for generations. Zashiko, our family ghost, who sent help when we needed it most. Baba had always promised that Zashiko would protect us. The powers of a house ghost were truly mighty. I wiped away my tears and stood fierce.

"Zashiko will come for me," I said, the words searing from my mouth into the freezing air. "She'll send help. Baba told me. I am never alone."

Cait barked into the night. "Zashiko? You think a house ghost will save you?" She let out a sly, rolling laugh.

"She's saved me before," I said, baring my fists. I guess I was planning to fight the Cait-weasel until Zashiko arrived - however long it took.

"She's a house ghost, you fool," Cait barked. "And

we are in the forest, no? We are far from your house now, Takeshita-san. Zashiko will not be interfering tonight."

And so that was that. I was betrayed, alone, and about to be eaten by a gang of mutant weasels in the guise of my best friend. My only hope was that I might freeze to death before Cait ripped me apart.

"She's coming! She's coming!"

A voice echoed from deep in the forest. I didn't swing around. I already knew whose voice it was. Even in the face of sudden death, it was annoying. Alex. Or more likely, the three-tailed Alex-fox.

"She's coming! I can see her," the Shape Shifter yelled, using Alex's voice perfectly.

Cait reacted instantly, hissing and slashing her nails through the air, then she jumped at me. I reacted on instinct, lunging to one side but landing awkwardly so that I rolled on my ankle. Pain shot through my leg and I tumbled to the ground, the first bit of luck I'd had all night. I felt the breeze of Cait's body as it whizzed over my head, grabbing at the empty air with her nails outstretched.

Thanks for the warning, fox-boy.

I wanted to yell "Her-who? Who's coming?", but figured I probably wasn't going to like the answer. Plus whoever she was could be a long while coming.

Foxes can see for hundreds and thousands of miles.

Cait recovered her balance and chirped, circling me where I lay. I scuttled backwards on my bottom, keeping the weight off my ankle. Cait didn't come any closer, but she wasn't letting me get away. She seemed distracted, sniffing at the air, tasting it with her tongue. Then she gave a screech and dropped to all fours, searching the night with glowing, white eyes.

I took a chance and scooted backwards, struggling up on one foot. Whoever 'she' was, I hoped she'd bring a spare jacket. I had started to shiver, as if I'd been trapped inside a freezer for weeks. The temperature was plunging and my body was throbbing with the cold. The tips of my fingers were as white as Cait's eyes. Even my blood seemed to have slowed.

And then I felt something tickling down my neck. A spider? A kiss? No. A tiny barb of ice. It was a snowflake.

I looked around. There were more. Flakes the size of coins began to fall from the sky. I felt like cheering, because suddenly I knew who was coming, who it was the fox had seen.

Only a powerful sorcerer could travel here at such speed, and turn a clear night to snow, and strike fear into the heart of a shape-changing fox like the one pretending to be Alex. Only a powerful sorcerer could outwit the kama itachi.

The yuki-onna. The Snow Woman. I swung round, searching the darkness for her perfect face.

I'd seen the yuki-onna once before, back when Cait and I had been searching for Mrs Okuda's headless body. She'd appeared just outside the window where Okuda's body had been hiding. She'd smiled at me, then disappeared in a single frosty breath. But that had been all we needed. After seeing her we'd found Okuda's body, fought Okuda's head, and survived to live another day. Now the yuki-onna was with us again, we'd survive this one too. The yuki-onna wasn't a house ghost, she wasn't bound by physical things. She was a woman of the snow. And now she was with us again.

I hardly saw the falling flakes. I hardly felt the cold. I stared into Cait's wild white eyes and whooped out loud. "She's coming, Cait. We're going to get you out."

CHAPTER
FIFTEEN

✾

A white glow leapt into the night from within the forest. It moved fast, like the headlights of a train, and we were right in its path.

The Cait-weasel reacted as if she'd been electrified. She reared up like a horse, tearing her arms through the air and slicing the night into shreds. She'd taken a break from trying to eat me and was now yipping and hissing at the growing light. I looked at her properly for the first time since the Sickle Weasels had taken her, and Cait's predicament began to sink in. My best friend's body had been completely overrun by kama itachi demons. A wave of bile gushed into my mouth but I swallowed it down. This was no time to be sick.

Something rippled through the night and I realised we were no longer alone. The yuki-onna towered over us, floating just above the ground, and she was more beautiful than anyone I had ever seen. I blinked, as if seeing all of her at once might hurt my eyes. Snow danced above her, sparkling in her eyes, and she wore a flowing, white kimono wrapped intricately around her.

There wasn't time to say thanks, or even hello.

The Cait-weasel lunged at the Snow Woman and the two collided, sending white sparks whirling into the sky. The yuki-onna was flung backwards, falling almost to the ground before a strange, hovering power seemed to scoop her up and plant her a few steps back, upright and still inches off the ground. She needed time to recover, though, and the Cait-weasel had spotted an opening. She moved in, teeth gnashing.

"Cait, no!"

My warning came too late. Cait grabbed a thick fold of the yuki-onna's kimono in her teeth and thrashed it around like a dog killing a rabbit, except the rabbit was the Snow Woman, perhaps our last and only hope. Cait tossed her back and forth as if she were as light as a feather.

With a wrenching sound, the silk kimono ripped

and Cait shook herself off balance, lurching sideways with a chunk of kimono still gripped in her teeth. The Snow Woman floated backwards, her invisible feet never touching the ground. She readjusted her kimono, folding the torn bit away and wrapping it right over left in her rush. The Cait-weasel spat the ruined silk to the floor and narrowed her eyes, preparing to lunge again.

"Miku," something hissed. "Over here!"

Having your name shouted out loud in the middle of a fight, especially when one of the fighters wants to eat you, is not the best idea in the world. Especially when the person shouting it is a weak-bellied filth-licking traitor. I swung round and sure enough, the aka-na-me was beckoning me. Typically, he'd backed well away from the action and was hiding in the doorway of the abandoned farmhouse.

"Get lost," I hissed, not wanting to draw further attention.

I needn't have worried. The Cait-weasel was otherwise occupied. She'd sprung again and this time the Snow Woman must have expected the attack. The tall woman stepped aside, waving one arm so the long sleeve of her kimono brushed Cait's head like a red flag at a bullfight. Cait roared and swung

round once again. Her eyes flared with the Sickle Weasels' white fire. She was going to pounce again.

"*Abunai*!" I cried. "Look out!"

"Miku!" the Filth Licker yelled. I looked and the red demon was still standing in the doorway, gesticulating wildly. "Over here," he hissed. "It's safer."

I had no wish to be indebted to a traitor, but I could see his point. Snow was still falling and my footprints were already outlined in white. The yuki-onna might be at home in these temperatures, but I didn't have a jacket and I'd be no good frozen solid as an ice block. Plus it might be harder for the Cait-weasel to fight in a confined space. If we could lure her inside the farmhouse, we might stand a chance.

"Yuki-onna-san," I called out, forcing my frozen face to form words. "The house."

But the white woman was too busy to hear me. She and the Cait-weasel were grappling, each holding the other's wrist in one hand. Cait was snapping her jaws, just out of reach of the yuki-onna's beautiful face. The Snow Woman's cheeks were as white as the snow that fell around us.

Icy air cut through my bare arms, and I was losing the feeling in my fingers and toes. If I didn't get somewhere warm soon, I reckoned I would pass out. I had to leave now, I had to trust that the yuki-onna could take care of herself.

I made a move towards the house, dragging my legs through snow that was now knee-deep in places. Behind me I could hear Cait's hissing and the snap of her teeth. The Snow Woman made no sound at all.

By the time I made it to the doorway of the farmhouse, my teeth were chattering. I didn't care that the only thing to greet me was a traitor who looked as if a large frog had collided with a red paint truck.

Between shivers and chatters, I formed the word I so desperately needed. "Inside."

The aka-na-me looked up from licking his arm. "Door is locked," he said. Tears were frozen across his cheeks and his eyes were as deep and soft as velvet. "You must hang on."

I didn't care that he'd been crying, that he'd betrayed me. I didn't care about anything except getting warm. My skin was blue and my arms and legs felt as if they were growing larger, freezing solid. They didn't feel like my own any more.

Then there was a sound, a wailing that carried across the blanket of snow. It was a cry like the wind's, as pale as a wisp of smoke. And then it was gone.

When I turned, the yuki-onna was gone and the

Cait-weasel was bounding through the snow towards me, her white eyes now rippling blood-red. In the morbid cold everything seemed to have slowed. I could feel each beat of my pulse, see individual flakes as they hung in the air. I watched Cait as she moved. She was on all fours, her body strangely fluid. The yuki-onna was nowhere to be seen.

Cait would be on to me in seconds. And I was too frozen to run.

I felt cold hands close around my body, their grip as strong as stone. The impact lifted me off the ground, and I waited for the pain, to feel the Cait-weasel's claws sinking in. But there was nothing, just stillness. I heard Cait hiss somewhere close, but still I felt nothing. So that answered my question about being eaten alive while freezing to death. It didn't hurt a bit. Before I could even feel relieved, I was off again, thrown upwards by the cold, clammy hands that gripped me. I stopped again. Then I was flung upwards once more. Again I stopped.

And that's when I opened my eyes. I seemed to be hovering in the air. Icy hands gripped me, but they weren't Cait's. She was below me, slashing and jumping at the air, still trying to reach me. And I was looking down on her, peering down at my own footsteps in the snow.

My vision blurred as we surged upwards, me and whoever belonged to the strong, cold hands that had me pinned. When we stopped moving again I got more of a look. They were strong, red hands. And below them, ugly clawed feet.

The aka-na-me smiled down at me, or at least I think he was smiling. It was hard to tell because his tongue was stuck to the wall of the farmhouse. He held me wrapped in his arms like an oversized baby. Beneath us, his clawed feet gripped the wall and the Cait-weasel seethed, well out of reach.

He jumped again, moving up the wall tongue-by-foot. I wanted to yell, to accuse him of betraying us, to tell him I knew about his plan with the fake sacred oil. Instead, my teeth chattered and my mouth wouldn't work. I bit my lip and tasted the warm tang of my own blood. Warm. It was actually warm. I licked my lip and heat seemed to gush from my split skin.

The warmth on my tongue flooded through me. My fingers began to move, my head cleared up. I could operate my mouth again and I opened it, planning to say something intelligent. All that came out was a yelp.

There was one more lurch upwards and then the

aka-na-me's grip loosened. *"Ki wo tsukete,"* I heard him say. "Be careful."

I looked around. The ground sloped away at my feet, still covered with snow, but Cait was nowhere to be seen. Then I realised: it wasn't the ground. Because we weren't on the ground. The Filth Licker had carried me to the roof.

CHAPTER
SIXTEEN

"You betrayed us." I glared at the aka-na-me demon. "You gave us oil laced with spirits, you led us into a trap."

The demon flushed even redder and licked at his feet, cleaning where they had touched the walls.

"Admit it. You work for them. You're one of the bad guys." I glowered , then realised that he had also rescued me from certain death.

The Filth Licker curled even smaller and kept licking. Bullying him would get me nowhere. I had to calm down. Plus I felt sorry for him. I was about three times his size, but he'd just carried me up a wall.

"Look, I'm sorry," I started again. "You saved my life by bringing me up here…"

The demon looked up. *"Shiranakatta,"* he said,

blinking sadly. "The oil, I did not know."

"What do you mean?"

"The keukegen." He licked an eyeball. "He said we were prisoners in the cleaning cupboard…"

Of course, the tiny, fur-ball demon, back at the shower block. Another of the fox's disguises.

"He said we were watched." The Filth Licker's voice cracked. "Night and day. But then you came, and you said I could be free." Tears were bulging from his eyeballs and he paused to lick them away.

"I never said you could be free," I retorted. "I didn't even know you were a prisoner."

"I only wanted to help," the Filth Licker wailed, lip trembling. More tears spurted from both eyes and our conversation paused while he mopped them up.

"But the keukegen? You said he was your pet."

"*Uso wo tsuita*," he wailed. "I lied. I was afraid. I didn't mean to hurt anyone." The tiny demon cringed. "He always told me what to say," he blubbered. "He told me in my head."

There was an almighty crash from beneath us. I peered over the edge. The Cait-weasel was staring up at us, her teeth bared. She had jumped up on to a windowsill and was scrabbling with bleeding nails for a grip on the wall.

"She's trying to climb," I gasped.

The aka-na-me shook his head, giving me a shy grin. For once he looked almost proud. "She cannot climb. She isn't a climber."

"But the kama itachi..."

"They cannot climb either." The Filth Licker gave me a shy grin. "Not in Cait's body."

I stared at him in wonder. "You saved us. We're safe up here." I looked around. The snow had stopped falling and light was coming into the sky. Sure, we couldn't stay on the roof forever, but it did buy us some time. The red demon was a genius. "What happened to the yuki-onna?" I asked. "And where's Alex? What about Mr James?"

The Filth Licker looked over the edge, into the forest. "Alex, I do not know. Mr James has been gone for over a week. But the kitsune Shape Shifter has run. His people will not be impressed. He will pay a heavy price."

"And the yuki-onna?"

"Who can say?" The Filth Licker licked along his feet again. "She comes and goes as she pleases."

And she never stayed long. Surely she wouldn't have deserted us? Perhaps she'd done her work already? "Is Cait cured?" I took another look. My friend was still hissing and barking and slashing with her nails, so that answered my question nice and quick. "OK. So now what?"

"Only you can say." The Filth Licker stopped licking and dipped his head in my direction. "You freed me, Takeshita-san. I am at your service."

I stared at the top of his head, aware that Cait's scrabbling noises beneath us were getting louder. Could I really trust him? "And you're sure about the oil, that you didn't know?"

He cringed. "The keukegen gave me that oil. I was tricked." He stopped to lick one arm. "He told me it was my uncle's. He told me it had mighty powers. I thought I was being so brave. I ran through the forest, past the hungry foxes and badgers, straight to you, Takeshita-san. I came to help." His little face trembled. "And instead I caused great trouble."

He was correct on that count. Would the Sickle Weasels' nest have burned with any other oil? Would their spirits have attacked Cait if the Filth Licker hadn't encouraged us to build that fire? But it was too late to worry about that. Spilt water will not return to its tray.

There was an awkward silence while I wondered what to say. Then I realised: the silence was wrong. Cait's hissing and barking had stopped. For a second everything was quiet, then with a whistling and gusting and raging, the winds started again. The Sickle Weasels' hurricane.

"Miku?" A tiny voice came from below. "Are you there?" The voice was Cait's. The real Cait's.

"Cait?" I held my breath and peeped over the edge, hardly daring to believe.

"Miku!" Cait's eyes were her own. Her mouth looked normal and her greenish tinge was gone. Even the blood was cleansed from her fingertips. And her relief was obvious. "Are you OK?"

Cait was back. I felt as if my favourite cake had flown right into my mouth. But there wasn't time to celebrate. The winds were churning in a familiar pattern. "Get somewhere safe," I warned her. "There's going to be a storm."

"I know," she said, and she looked at the sky. "You've got to run, Miku. I know them now. The kama itachi are coming for you."

Run isn't exactly the best course of action when you're on a rooftop, but I got the general idea. Above us the Sickle Weasels had split into three separate spirits and were once again whirling and swooping and slashing. Things didn't look good.

"They want you most of all," the Filth Licker interrupted. "That's why I chose the roof."

I stared at the demon. "But they can fly, and we're

trapped up here."

"*Chigaimasu.*" The demon shook his head. "Not so. It's my plan." He grinned. "When they were down there," he pointed, "Cait's body could not climb to here. So they set her free."

Cait being free was certainly a fabulous part of his plan. But another important part was missing. Sickle Weasels were whirling overhead and we were stuck on the roof of an abandoned farmhouse. "And tell me again how we're not trapped?"

"The chimney," he said.

"The chimney?"

He grinned and jumped on the spot.

I couldn't believe it. That was his plan? We were just going to pop down the chimney and everything would be OK? "I'm not Santa Claus."

"Santa who?"

"Oh, forget it." This chimney plan might not be foolproof, but at least it could buy Cait some time to escape.

I stared into the whirlwind. Even in the dark I could spot glints of steel as the Weasels slashed through the night. On the roof the air was still calm. We were right at the centre of their storm.

"Fine." I decided on the spot. "I'll take the chimney. But not you."

The Filth Licker looked hurt.

"Not you," I repeated. "You go with Cait. You have to keep her safe."

"But the winds." The demon looked afraid. "I am too little, too easily blown away."

"Stick together," I said. "Literally. With Cait's weight and your sticky limbs, you'll be OK. Climb a tree, take cover, do something. Just don't let them get her again." I took a deep breath, staring at the chimney.

"*Wakatta*." The Filth Licker nodded. He understood, and at once became very calm. "I will look after her, you have my word." He dipped his head to me. "*Ganbatte kudasai*, Takeshita-san. Go well."

And then he was gone, over the edge of the roof and into the storm. I hoped he'd find Cait and that they'd get to safety. All at once, I felt horribly and incredibly alone.

CHAPTER SEVENTEEN

I stared into the black nothing that was the chimney's inside. So it all came down to this. We'd walked through the night, faced a forest of sprites and demons, been possessed by weasels and replaced by foxes. Well, some of us had been possessed by weasels and replaced by foxes. I was still safe. Except that now I had to jump down a chimney.

But, I reasoned with myself, surely that couldn't be too bad. The farmhouse was old and its chimney was massive, as wide and deep as a well. I tried not to think about when it had last been used, probably decades ago. There could be hungry spiders living inside, or nests of bats. What if I got stuck halfway down? I swallowed, imagining the Sickle Weasels' blades.

Above me the kama itachi were slashing and spiralling through their storm. Their whirlwind was reaching its peak, but at the centre of their storm, a strange stillness was building around me. The tornado would soon invert, sucking me straight into their blades.

Well, if they wanted it easy, they had another think coming. I wasn't going to be served to a bunch of Sickle Weasels like tea in a pot. I climbed up and over the edge of the chimney, letting my legs dangle into the blackness within. A plan was forming in my head. This chimney might be big enough for me to get down, but what about the Sickle Weasels? What about their long, steel blades?

The blades. That was it.

I lowered my body into the chimney and hung there, dangling by my fingertips.

Then I felt the winds change around me. The storm was inverting. My long hair was sucked up around my face and the sleeves of my shirt flew up into the vacuum. But I didn't care. I was grinning. The Sickle Weasels were too late.

I took a deep breath. I kept a memory of smiling Kazu in my head. And then I let go.

At once I was tumbling down through the blackness and the suffocating air. I bounced off the insides of the chimney, buffeted from side to side, each impact stealing my breath and ripping my clothes. I wished for my jacket, for some protection, but all I could do was just curl my bare arms around my body and tuck my head in tight. I felt like a human torpedo, racing through space towards earth.

A few hurtling, screaming, utterly black seconds later, I popped out of the chimney's other end, gasping and bleeding into a storm of ash and dust and blindness. The fireplace. And at least there wasn't a fire.

I scrambled to get out. If my hunch was right, the Sickle Weasels would be coming after me the fastest way possible, and the same way as me. Straight down the chimney.

Only they had something I didn't have: massive scythes. Their long steel blades wouldn't fit down the chimney. They'd have to retract their sickles and come down unarmed, hopefully one at a time.

I crawled from the fireplace and looked around for a weapon. A fire poker. A bit of wood. Anything. When they arrived I could knock them off, one by one, before they had a chance to re-arm their blades

But what I saw left me cold. The farmhouse floor wasn't layered with dust like the fireplace had been. Instead it was carpeted with furs, tiny furs. The skins of dead mice, rats, rabbits. The whole thing was one massive nest for the kama itachi. And they'd been laying. The nest we'd burned earlier must have been a decoy, a few sacrificial eggs designed to lure us in. The main event was in here, where the entire floor was pulsing. There must have been hundreds of eggs, all laid in interlocking circles, all beating to the same rhythm.

I didn't have time to catch my breath, let alone grab a weapon. There was a puff of ash from the chimney and the first Sickle Weasel emerged from the fireplace. I spun round, but too slowly. With a screech of steel on steel, the Weasel extended long blades from his paws. Each blade was nearly half as long as me.

"Now we wait for my brothers." And we didn't wait long.

There were two puffs of ash, two more shrieks of steel on steel. Then the three of them stood there, side-by-side in a deadly line, each with their shining blades at the ready.

"How do you like our little nest, Takeshita-san," the lead Weasel asked. I stared. It was the first time I'd seen the kama itachi up close. Except for their size they looked almost normal, like furry pets with soft button noses and shiny round eyes. And teeth as sharp as razors, and hairy bodies wriggling with delight. I was pinned like a rat in their trap. "We're preparing a feast," their leader snarled. "Aren't you glad you could join us?"

The smaller Weasels clucked like chickens, bouncing and wriggling with joy.

"You can't eat me," I bluffed, hoping I was correct. "Take a look around. We're inside a house. I'm protected here. Zashiko protects me."

"Perhaps she protects *you*, Takeshita-san," said the Weasel, eyeing my grazed and bleeding limbs. I held both arms self-consciously. My cuts and scrapes stung like crazy, but dust and ash had covered most of the blood. The Sickle Weasel clucked, running the blades of one front paw back and forth across his tail with a sound like sharpening knives. "But she doesn't protect him."

I looked where he was pointing, and gasped. There, curled asleep on one of the few remaining bits of spare floor, was Alex.

He looked well, healthier than before. His black eye was gone, his pearl pendant was back, and the oily stains on his shirt and hands were completely erased. He looked as if he'd never even entered the forest. Then it twigged. Perhaps he hadn't. The real Alex could have been sleeping like a baby all night long. We could have been travelling with the shape-changing fox ever since we left camp.

The lead Weasel whistled. "What do you think? Our friendly fox arranged everything, delivering you straight to our blades, and the boy as well. What do you call it in English? Meals on Legs?"

"You can't hurt him," I bluffed. "Zashiko protects all who are with me."

The Weasel whistled a laugh and his brothers shrieked and bounced around him. "You both offered stories to the Hyaku Monogatari, so we cannot kill him, and we cannot kill you. But he can kill you, Takeshita-san." The Weasel clucked and slashed his blades through the air. "We will enter the boy and he can kill you for us. Then your blood will fuel our power. And when our children are born, even the yuki-onna cannot stop us."

He waved one sickled paw at the floor of pulsating eggs and the Weasels' shrieking grew wilder. "Be ready, my brothers," the lead Weasel ordered. "And be careful. We don't want to disturb the children." He smiled softly at the eggs, then turned his beady, black eyes back to me.

The yuki-onna? So she was still alive. But why had she left us?

I didn't have time for questions. The smaller Weasels began whirling together in a tight circle,

moving so fast they became a blur. A column of air began to orbit around them, forming a whirlwind that swayed on the spot, a pillar of spinning sound and light.

The lead Weasel bared his needle teeth at me, a kind of farewell smile, then turned and leapt into the centre of his brothers' whirling storm. At once it seemed to spin faster, whizzing and buzzing like a loose electrical wire. The storm gave a jerk, then began to move, weaving its way across the floor, skipping lightly through the nest without so much as nudging an egg. It was headed for the back corner, where Alex was lying.

"Alex!" I screamed over the roar of the winds, trying to warn him, hoping he could run.

But he didn't stir. I guessed the sleep he was in was anything but natural.

The Sickle Weasels' storm arced like lightning, sending a beam of wind and spirit energy striking down at Alex like a fist.

The beam bounced off him, rebounding into the roof with a shriek. I screamed and Alex jolted a couple of feet into the air, then fell back to the ground, limp. Was he dead? But his eyes twitched and his chest was moving. Okuda's pearl, where it hung on his neck, was glowing bright and angry into the night.

Again the kama itachi sent their fury upon Alex. They were aiming to possess him just as they had possessed Cait. They would use him to attack me, just as Cait had attacked me. Only this time there was nowhere to run. I was trapped. Gift-wrapped in blood and dust, right inside their nest.

Again the Sickle Weasels' storm arced towards Alex. Again it was rejected, reflected from his chest with an energy that lifted his sleeping body into the air. The pearl was so bright it burned my eyes just to look at it. Even with my eyes closed I could hear the screech of the Weasels' blades, the ferocity of their attack. I heard them whirl faster and faster, felt the very air become electric. Then, through covered eyes, I watched as they arced their storm once again towards Alex. There was no way he could withstand this power.

KA-BOOM!

There was a rocketing explosion as the arc of the storm collided with the pearl around Alex's neck. Alex was shot into the air and in an instant the pearl erupted. The room flashed white, sending sheets of blinding light through the air.

CHAPTER EIGHTEEN

The kama itachi's storm smacked into the ceiling, crashed into the floor, then rebounded back up to the ceiling, out of control in the wake of the explosion. The pulsing eggs erupted; shards of ceiling and singed furs were scattered like shrapnel. And Alex hadn't moved. He lay where he had landed, still dangerously close to the storm. The pearl had disappeared, exploded into a thousand lights. Now he had nothing to protect him.

I couldn't watch any longer. I had to get out of there, and take Alex with me. If the Filth Licker could carry me up the side of a house, the least I could do was to drag Alex out of the storm's way. I leapt across the first circle of eggs, racing to the spot where he lay. I felt the Sickle Weasels' storm rage over my head, then blast into the wall beside me. Alex murmured something in his sleep but didn't wake.

Shards of light from the pearl's explosion were still twinkling, but their power was dying. How much longer did we have?

The storm came humming towards me and I ducked, then dived to the floor, smashing a bunch of eggs as I crashed to the ground.

I lay still for a moment, then took off like a sprinter, scrambling so my hands could keep up with the pumping of my legs. More eggs exploded as the storm collided with the space where I'd been. Was their aim improving?

Alex was only metres away now. Something flashed in the corner of my eye and I lunged sideways, landing on one shoulder with a squelch of smashing eggshells. The storm ricocheted off the wall exactly where I had been a moment before.

"Alex!" I cried out, trying to wake him. There was no point in me trying to carry him out of this mess if he could walk on his own. But he didn't even open his eyes. Trust him to be sleeping in a crisis.

I lunged again, sliding through the animal furs and broken eggshells to land at Alex's feet. And I made it. So that was halfway. Now we just had to get out.

Looking around the room, my heart sank. It looked as if someone had been making the world's biggest omelette and then stirred in a carload of dead mice. And still the storm hadn't stopped. It was whirling on the far side of the farmhouse, blocking the door and two windows. I heaved Alex into my arms. It took all my strength and I could only lift his shoulders. The rest of him hung limp on the floor.

I dropped him and he slumped to the floor. "Alex, wake up!"

He muttered something but didn't stop snoring. The storm bounced back in our direction, switching from left to right across the room like a laser show.

I tried to heave Alex higher but nearly dropped him again. The storm was close now, really close. I could smell frying eggs and singeing fur as it whizzed back and forth. "Alex!" I slapped him with one hand, but he just sighed in his sleep and turned away. We were never going to make it.

Our only hope was to hide. I pushed Alex further into the corner, sliding his body on a sledge of slippery furs. I was desperate, hoping that the storm would pass over us, or that the Sickle Weasels might explode before they even got to us. I shoved Alex right against the wall and piled tiny furs all around him, then I sat on top of him and tried to look relaxed.

So that was my masterplan. So much for having secret powers. I was terrified, unable to think straight, and sitting on one of my classmates. I guess I was hoping the Sickle Weasels might think Alex was some sort of lovely furry sofa. Maybe they'd miss him altogether.

Then I turned to face their whirlwind.

The storm was still spiralling, but it was hovering in the centre of the room, not shifting from its spot. Had the Sickle Weasels run out of steam?

Then an angry hissing and clucking came from inside the storm. Followed by the scrape of metal on metal, knives sharpening knives. And at that moment I realised. I was horribly wrong.

"Takeshita-san," the lead Weasel's voice boomed over the whirl of their wind. "You have destroyed us. Destroyed our nest."

"No," I blathered. "That wasn't me, that was the pearl. I haven't done a thing."

"Our future is gone…" The voice echoed from the storm. I watched as the tornedo gathered itself into a spear and then an arrow and then a sword.

No. This wasn't the way it was supposed to happen. "But you said. You can't kill me, remember? We're bound together." I was rambling. "You said my words were part of the hundred, the Hyaku Monogatari, you said..."

"What we said is past, before this destruction," the voice boomed. "We can no longer waste time. We will not play by her rules. We will have your blood now."

The storm leapt through the air as if it were lightning, arcing straight for me, and for Alex beneath me. I didn't have time to think. I threw up both hands, hoping to protect my face from the Sickle Weasels' power.

I felt a jolt, then everything went quiet.

CHAPTER NINETEEN

When I opened my eyes the room was strangely still, and completely devastated. It was splattered with raw egg and stank of burned fur. Plaster and brick were falling from the smashed ceiling and walls. Beneath me Alex stirred in his sleep but still did not wake. And there was no sign of the Sickle Weasels. The whole room seemed empty.

Then something tiny moved at my feet.

I stood to take a better look. It was a mouse, a tiny fieldmouse. It looked right at me with glowing white in its eyes, then it squeaked twice, slashing its paws through the air.

The Sickle Weasels? Was that even possible?

The mouse bared its teeth and tried to attack my shoe. I heard the screech of metal on metal and

I realised. The Weasels had missed. Somehow the kama itachi had channelled their spirits into the furry skin of a mouse instead of into me. I balanced on one leg, pinning the wriggling skin to the floor with my spare foot. The mouse screeched, face green with fury and legs scrabbling to be free. But now what? I could kill it just by snapping its neck with my shoe, but somehow that didn't feel right. I could box it up, keep it in a jar?

The mouse hissed at me, foam forming in the corners of its mouth. Whatever I did, it would have to be quick. The Sickle Weasels could abandon this mouse in an instant and begin once again to build their whirlwind.

I swallowed, preparing to stab down with my foot, to crush its little body like a swollen berry.

The mouse shrieked again, and on the other side of the farmhouse, a door burst open. A white fox bounded in, red mouth open and sharp teeth at the ready. The fox ran straight at me and I reacted at once, releasing the mouse and backing up against the wall.

I didn't have time to count its tails. I got as far as seven before the fox swept the mouse into its jaws and crunched hard. The bones of the mouse cracked into a thousand pieces and I swear I could hear the shrieking of Weasels.

I stared goggle-eyed at the white fox while it chewed and then swallowed.

"*Shitsurei shimashita*," it said, looking around the shattered room. "Sorry. I think I'm a little late."

I couldn't believe it. "A little late?"

The fox burped. "Sickle Weasels," it said. "Never a favourite. Now, I heard something about a lost boy?"

I sat back down, staring. This fox was different from the one that had replaced Alex. For a start it was smaller, a regular fox size, plus it was pure white and older, with twice as many tails. "He's here," I said, pointing beneath me.

"Oh," said the fox. "I thought that was a sofa."

With a flick of his tails the fox's features melted before me. His fox body grew taller and older, his face rounder, his nose less pronounced. In seconds the fox that had stood before me was gone. In its place was an old man with white hair and wrinkled skin. "Can you lend me a hand?" the man asked. "He looks heavy."

If I hadn't seen it, I would never have believed it. I only wished Baba could have seen it too.

"Sure," I said, trying to pretend I did this kind of thing every day. I held Alex's legs, and the old man heaved on his arms, and together we carted our sleeping friend through the destroyed room and out of

the farmhouse, into the bright light of the morning.

We lowered Alex to the freezing ground, still dusted with melting snow, but even then he didn't stop snoring.

"You know, I had that mouse under control," I said, feeling proud but strangely shy.

"I know you did, Takeshita Miku," said the old man, smiling. "I know you did."

From across the field I heard a welcome cry. "Miku! And it's Alex!" Cait ran towards us, with the Filth Licker hopping along behind her.

When I looked back at the old man, he was gone. In his place the white fox twitched his whiskers. "Thank you, Takeshita Miku," it said. "I am sorry for the role my people played in this event. The one responsible will be tracked down. He is no longer any fox of ours."

"I'm pleased to know that," I said, not knowing what else to say. For some reason I gave the fox a deep bow.

"He won't come any closer," Cait interrupted. She and the Filth Licker had stopped some metres back. The red demon was quaking in his boots, refusing to move forward.

"Shape Shifters," I explained to the white fox. "He's not a fan."

The fox raised itself up on its hind legs. "Aka-na-me-san," it said, addressing the red demon. "You have been very brave today. You have risked much to come here, to stand by the Takeshita clan, and for that we are grateful."

The Filth Licker relaxed a little but didn't step forward. He didn't look keen to make friends.

"You have my word," continued the white fox. "You will be safe in the forest. The Shape Shifters will not eat you. We are on the same side now."

The little demon looked at Cait, who smiled, then he did a little hop. "Very brave," I heard him whisper. "I have been very brave."

"Are we safe now?" I asked carefully. "My family, my friends, my classmates? Is it over? And what happened to the yuki-onna?"

"What happens between other clans is not our affair," the fox replied. "We are Shape Shifters. Not mortals, not demons."

"But what about Alex?"

The white fox peered down at Alex where he slept. "The boy is unharmed. He will wake from a wonderful dream."

I stared at Alex. "When will he wake?"

"Who can tell?"

"Isn't he under some sort of spell?"

The white fox snuffled, his eyes twinkling. "Not at all. We can impersonate humans, certainly, but we cannot make them sleep."

Typical. So Alex really had slept through the entire thing. "What happens next?" I asked. "What about Oscar and Mr James? What about these powers I'm supposed to have?"

"You used your powers today," said the fox, "and used them well. Your grandmother would have been proud."

"You knew Baba?"

"Better than you can imagine." The fox ruffled its thick white coat. "She was a wonderful friend."

I felt my eyes grow wide and wet. Baba would have loved to see all this stuff.

Footsteps crunched through the melting snow as Cait and the Filth Licker came closer. "Are you OK?" Cait asked. "You look like you've been busy."

I looked down at my scraped arms and filthy shirt. Dust, raw egg, ash, blood. Cait grinned at me and I grinned back. The old Cait had returned. "I'm going to need a long shower," I said.

The Filth Licker bounced up and down on the spot. "At your service, Takeshita-san. At your service." His hairy tongue quivered in and out.

"Erm, thanks." I smiled at the little demon. "Maybe

I'll clean me, and *you* could clean the shower?"

The demon grinned. "My pleasure."

Cait stared down at Alex's sleeping body. "Alex," she said, smiling goofily. "And he's OK?"

I nodded. "Just sleeping." I looked back at the white fox. "What about Oscar? Will he be all right?"

"Oscar?" The white fox looked confused.

"He has tōfu-kozō poisoning. Please tell me there's a cure."

"Ah," the fox nodded. "A large man, big of belly? Very smelly with the tōfu-kozō rash."

"You mean Mr James?"

The fox's ears twitched. "The caretaker fellow. He developed the rash last week, left just before your bus arrived. Straight to the hospital, I think."

So that's what had happened to Mr James. "There's also another one, a boy called Oscar."

"They are both called Oscar?"

"No." I tried to explain. "The man is Mr James, the boy is Oscar."

"Well." The fox twitched its nose. "They both need a good shower. But your demon friend can help with that. I've never known a tōfu-kozō rash that couldn't be cured by an aka-na-me."

The Filth Licker bounced up and down on the spot. "Tōfu-kozō rash? Really?" His tongue zapped

195

in and out. "I haven't tasted that in years."

I grinned. "It's that simple?"

And the white fox twinkled his eyes.

I nudged Alex with my foot. "As soon as this one wakes up, we'll organise for you and Oscar to have a little get-together back at camp," I said to the Filth Licker. "And then I guess we'll have to visit Mr James in hospital." I wasn't sure how we'd explain the little red demon, or whether Mr James would be keen to be licked all over, but I sure hoped the real Mr James was a better cook than the shape-changing fox.

The Filth Licker hopped about like a frog and thumped his huge one-clawed foot. "Awesome. That will be awesome."

Cait was staring down at Alex again, a dopey smile on her face. "He looks so peaceful when he's sleeping."

"Doesn't he!" I grinned.

CHAPTER TWENTY

The Filth Licker's wet, furry tongue rolled up the side of Alex's sleeping face. Alex's eyes sprang open and he sat up, looking around wildly. "What's going on? Where am I?"

"You need cleaning," I explained. "You've been sleeping. And now you are awake."

Cait giggled and the Filth Licker licked again, this time covering Alex's forehead and taking his floppy fringe with it. Alex spluttered, struggling to get to his feet on the wet grass. "Gross. That'll do, thanks all the same."

"You're welcome." The Filth Licker did a little bow and Cait giggled again.

Alex wiped a hand across his face and looked pleasantly surprised. "No drool," he said. "Nice."

The Filth Licker nodded. *"Deshō."* He looked pleased.

Alex looked around, confused. "So where are we? I thought we were going hunting for a super-demon." He looked again at the Filth Licker. "You. Here. But I thought you weren't coming?"

"I walked," said the demon. "I have been very brave."

Alex stood up, looking around at the abandoned farm, the melting snow, the dark forest on the edge of the field. "What's going on? What happened?"

"We're at the farm," I explained. "It's over. And *you* slept through everything."

Alex scratched his head and then reached for his pearl. His eyes grew panicked. "It's gone," he said. "My pearl. It's gone." He swung round, searching on the ground with his hands.

"Don't worry," I grinned. "It kind of exploded. I think it saved your life."

"What?" Now it was Alex's turn to look bewildered.

"Want me to pull your hair?" Cait offered, grinning. "It might help you to remember."

"What're you talking about?" Alex looked bemused, squinting at the sun on the melting snow.

"It's been a long night," I said. "We can explain on the way back."

"Back?"

"Yeah, we're on school camp, remember?" Cait laughed. "We've probably missed breakfast and they might even be missing us. Plus I really want to try that campfire cooking."

Alex nodded slowly.

"Just one question..." I said.

"Sure," he mumbled, still scratching his head.

"How much do you remember? About last night?"

Alex was silent for a minute. "We saw the puff-ball," he began, sounding confused. "We met you," he pointed at the Filth Licker, who stamped his foot in approval. "We made a plan to leave and headed to the cabins..."

"And then what?"

"Then..." He blinked in the sun. "Then Mr James came," he said. "To my cabin. No, wait. It was a fox, a brown fox. No, wait, it can't have been a fox. Because it could talk, so, and... no...." He stopped, a little dazed. "I can't quite remember. Hey, wasn't there a fox here earlier, a white one?"

We looked around. The white fox had gone. His paw prints headed back into the forest, back to his people.

"There was," I said, "but he's gone. He's preparing our way home."

I sighed with relief. I was starving and bleeding and smelt like burnt egg, but things were looking up. Everyone was in control of their own bodies. Everyone would be cured of their stinky rashes. And we'd overcome an evil plan to create a demon empire. A good night's work.

I looked around. Alex and Cait were smiling, but the Filth Licker's face had dropped "What's the matter?" I asked. "You should be happy. You saved our lives."

He gave his arm a long lick. "Home," he said. "Where will I go?"

"Back to your home," I said. "You're free now." When he didn't look up, I thought a little longer. "Where is your home exactly?"

The demon answered between licks. "I don't have a home. I have been prisoner in the shower block for so long." His big eyes welled up.

"But what about your relatives? You could always live with one of them."

"Or me," Alex said. "We've got space. You like the city?"

The aka-na-me stopped licking. "The city?"

"Sure. Heaps of bathrooms there. You should see mine. It's filthy. Mum keeps telling me to clean it, but I never do." Alex grinned and the Filth Licker's tongue began to dart. "There's always mildew on the tiles." Alex warmed to his subject. "And there's this grey stuff all round the bottom of the bath. And the ceiling. It's mould metropolis up there."

The demon began to thump his foot. "Are you sure? Could I really?"

"Alex," I began, not sure I was hearing things right. "Do you really think you can have a filth-licking demon to stay in your house?"

"Sure." Alex nodded, his floppy fringe bouncing. "Mum would never need to know. I've even got a spare bunk you could sleep in."

The demon hopped about on the spot. "Is that really OK?" he asked. "And don't worry about the bunk. I prefer the bath."

"That's totally perfect," Alex said, "because our bathroom's available. No one's sleeping in it. It'll be all yours."

The demon did a mad little dance, bouncing so hard he looked as if he was drumming in a festival.

"So that seals it." I grinned. "Alex will never have to clean again. Unlike me." I pulled a chunk of cold egg out of my hair. "Let's get back to camp. I really need that shower."

"You sure stink," Alex said, sniffing me. "What did you do? Bathe in rotten egg? There's no way I'm sitting next to you on the way home."

"I'll sit next to you, Alex," Cait said shyly.

"Sweet," Alex crowed. "Oscar and Miku Mouse can stink up their seat together."

Argh. I lunged at Alex and he skipped out of the way.

"Come on!" I laughed. "We better get a move on. It's a long way back to camp."

Read an extract from Miku's third,
brilliant *Takeshita Demons* adventure

MONSTER MATSURI

CHAPTER ONE

My hands were sweaty and I realised I was clinging
to the bag. "Ready?" I whispered.

Cait nodded, and Alex curved both hands round
his body as if they were blades.

We were standing outside Alex's bedroom door,
and I was so close to Alex I could hear him breathe.
A few months ago this would have been my worst
nightmare, and I guess Alex would have felt the
same way. There was a big sign on his door that said
PRIVATE, NO GIRLS in enormous, black letters.

Cait was standing next to me in what she called
her work uniform: jeans and a jumper, one size too
small, so the enemy wouldn't get a good grip. She
looked ready for action.

Alex looked ready for bed. He was still in his
pyjamas.

I cleared my throat. "Alex, are you ready?"

Alex circled his hands through the air, then he
nodded without taking his eyes off the door. Our
team was set.

I swallowed, and started the countdown.

"One..."

More about Japanese Demons

Better known as *yokai* (妖怪), supernatural demons have featured in Japanese fairy tales and folklore for centuries. Many hundreds of *yokai* exist: some came originally from China while others sprang up to explain spooky stories or strange happenings. Scholars have been cataloguing *yokai* species in encyclopedias and databases since the 1770s.

Yokai are still popular in modern Japan: they have restaurant dishes named after them, statues sold of them, books written about them. They star in manga comics and movies, are used to advertise banks and beer, and might still be blamed when something strange goes bump in the night.

The Japanese characters used to write *yokai* mean 'bewitching' and 'suspicious', and the word can refer to all kinds of supernatural spirits: goblins, ghosts, monsters and more. *Yokai* can be bringers of luck or harbingers of doom, clippers of hair or shakers of beans. They can be good, evil, or just plain strange.

Only one thing is certain about *yokai*: one is probably watching you right now!

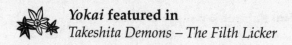

Yokai **featured in**
Takeshita Demons – The Filth Licker

Akaname **(Filth Licker)** 垢嘗

Great news: if you don't clean your bathroom, the *akaname* will. He has red, frog-like skin, a long hairy tongue and a fondness for slime, mould and rot. He likes to lick grimy bathrooms until they sparkle.

Ashi-magari **(Leg-turner)** 足曲がり

The *ashi-magari* is a mischievous spirit that comes out at night to trip you up and slow you down. You might feel it winding around your ankles, or tugging at your legs.

Betobeto-san **(Mr Footsteps)** べとべとさん

Ever had the feeling that someone was following you? Or have you heard footsteps but turned around to see no one was there? Perhaps it was *Betobeto-san*. He's quite shy, so try standing to the side of the road and inviting him to go ahead.

Hitodama **(Human souls)** 人魂

If a person dies, their spirit can soar to the sky in the form of a fireball. When the fireball falls back to earth, it splatters everything in slime. *Hitodama* can be orange or blue or white, and often appear just before a sick person passes away.

Kama itachi **(Sickle Weasels)** 鎌鼬

Whirling with the winds and slicing through the night, the Sickle Weasels work in teams of three to slash at their enemies using long sickle blades that extend from their paws.

Keukegen **(Fluffy thing)** 毛羽毛現

Small and fluffy doesn't always equal cute and friendly. A *keukegen* looks like a small, furry dog, but it spreads disease and prefers to live in dark, damp places.

Kitsune (Fox) 狐

Young *kitsune* look like ordinary foxes, but the older they are, the more tails they grow, and the more powerful they become. When they have lived for a hundred years, they can change shape, even into human form. White foxes are linked to Inari, the god of rice. The fox's favourite food is fried tofu.

Kodama (Tree spirit) 木魂

Kodama live inside ancient trees, mimicking the sounds of the forest and causing echoes to bounce through the woods. Their trees are often ringed with a sacred rope called a shimenawa. If you cut down a kodama's tree, you're in for some very bad luck.

Noppera-bō (Faceless ghost) のっぺら坊

Is the person sitting next to you who you think they are? *Noppera-bō* pretend to be other people, and they love to make trouble. When you least expect it their features can disappear, melting away to leave their face as empty as a blank page.

Nukekubi (Cut-throat) 抜首

During the day you might mistake this *yokai* for a normal person, but be warned. At night, while its body is sleeping, its head can detach and fly around hunting for delicious things to eat (like children and puppy dogs).

Nure-onna (Woman of the Wet) 濡女

With the torso of a woman and the body of a snake, this *yokai* has wicked claws and a long, forked tongue. She's strong enough to crush a tree in the coils of her massive tail.

O-kubi (Big throat) 大首

If you're ever staring up at the sky and spot an enormous head in the clouds, watch out! Spotting an *o-kubi* usually means something awful is just around the corner…

Oni (Ogre) 鬼

Oni are famous for their mean looks and nasty personalities.
They have bad hair, poor dress sense and spiky horns. And
they like to eat people, which makes them very unpopular.

Satori (Mind-reader) 覚

He looks like a monkey and he smells like a monkey. But he
can also read your thoughts. The satori prefers to live in the
mountains and can only be conquered if you empty your mind.

Suna-kake-baba (Sand-throwing woman) 砂かけ婆

Living high in the treetops of a lonely forest, the *suna-kake-baba*
is a grumpy old lady who sprinkles sand on people as they
walk by underneath.

Tōfu-kozō (Tofu Monk) 豆腐小僧

The *tōfu-kozō* is a monk who wanders quiet country roads
carrying a plate of fresh tofu. Although it looks delicious,
the tofu is cursed, and those who eat it will start to rot.

Yamabiko (Ghostly valley echo) 幽谷響

Don't you hate it when someone echoes everything you say?
That's exactly what the *yamabiko* does. It lives in the mountains
and pretends to be a real echo.

Yuki-onna (Snow Woman) 雪女

Tall, pale and icily beautiful, this *yokai* is a spirit of the snow.
She leaves no footprints, preferring to float above the ground,
and she can disappear in a puff of cold mist.

Zashiki-warashi (House ghost) 座敷童

This mischievous *yokai* haunts houses and usually appears
as a child. If your house is haunted by a *zashiki-warashi*,
count yourself lucky, but take good care of it. If your house
ghost ever chooses to leave you, your luck will quickly end.

CRISTY BURNE

became fascinated with Japanese folklore and
the supernatural *yokai* – demons – which are
very much a part of Japanese culture, when she
was working in Japan as a teacher and editor.
Her first novel, *Takeshita Demons*, won the 2009
Frances Lincoln Diverse Voices Award, jointly
run and administered by Seven Stories in Newcastle
upon Tyne. It was selected by Book Trust for
Booked Up 2010 and was Blue Peter's Book of the
Month in January, 2011. It is also available as an
audio book (Frances Lincoln, £10.99).
A third novel in the *Takeshita Demons* series,
Monster Matsuri, will be published in June 2012.
Cristy Burne lives with her family in Perth,
Western Australia.

To find out more about the author and
Takeshita Demons, visit her blog:
cristyburne.wordpress.com, or visit
www.franceslincoln.com/takeshitademons